"I'm here to pick up my son,"
Pixie announced stiffly, her slim
shoulders rigid. "I'm sorry
you've been dragged into this...
er, situation."

There he stood, tall, poised, predatory dark eyes locked on her like grappling hooks seeking purchase in her tender skin. He was angry, suspicious, everything she didn't want to be forced to deal with, but even in that mood, she wasn't impervious to how gorgeous he was. And while still being that aware of his movie-star-hot looks annoyed her, it also reminded her of how very strange it was that she could ever have conceived a child with a man so far out of her league.

That night they had been together so briefly loomed like a distant and surreal fantasy in the back of her mind, and her face heated with mortification because *that* night was the very last thing she wanted to think about in his presence.

"You need to come in, take a seat and explain what you describe as a 'situation' to me," Tor said coolly, watching her like a hawk.

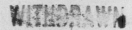

Innocent Christmas Brides

All the billionaire wants for Christmas...is her!

Billionaire half brothers Tor Sarantos and Sevastiano Cantarelli are famed the world over for their wealth, power and looks. Yet a dark family secret divides them.

It will take the strength and support of two very unique women for this family rivalry to be healed... in time for Christmas!

Tor's life is turned upside down by Pixie's bombshell in

A Baby on the Greek's Doorstep

Available now

When Sev meets innocent Amy, all bets are off!

Christmas Babies for the Italian

Coming next month

Indulge in this sparkling Christmas duet by *USA TODAY* bestselling author Lynne Graham!

Lynne Graham

A BABY ON THE
GREEK'S DOORSTEP

HARLEQUIN®
PRESENTS®

Recycling programs
for this product may
not exist in your area.

ISBN-13: 978-1-335-14889-6

A Baby on the Greek's Doorstep

Copyright © 2020 by Lynne Graham

This edition published by arrangement with Harlequin Books S.A.

For questions and comments about the quality of this book,
please contact us at CustomerService@Harlequin.com.

Harlequin Enterprises ULC
22 Adelaide St. West, 40th Floor
Toronto, Ontario M5H 4E3, Canada
www.Harlequin.com

Printed in U.S.A.

Lynne Graham was born in Northern Ireland and has been a keen romance reader since her teens. She is very happily married to an understanding husband who has learned to cook since she started to write! Her five children keep her on her toes. She has a very large dog who knocks everything over, a very small terrier who barks a lot and two cats. When time allows, Lynne is a keen gardener.

Books by Lynne Graham

Harlequin Presents

The Greek's Blackmailed Mistress
The Italian's Inherited Mistress
Indian Prince's Hidden Son

Conveniently Wed!

The Greek's Surprise Christmas Bride

One Night With Consequences

His Cinderella's One-Night Heir

Billionaires at the Altar

The Greek Claims His Shock Heir
The Italian Demands His Heirs
The Sheikh Crowns His Virgin

Cinderella Brides for Billionaires

Cinderella's Royal Secret
The Italian in Need of an Heir

Visit the Author Profile page
at Harlequin.com for more titles.

CHAPTER ONE

TOR SARANTOS IGNORED his security head's frown at the news that he would require neither his car nor his usual bodyguards that evening.

'You know what day this is.' Tor said simply. 'I go out… I go alone.'

'With all due respect,' the older man began heavily, 'in your position, it is not safe.'

'Duly noted,' Tor breathed very drily. 'But it is what I do, as you well know.'

Every year without fail for the past five years, Tor had gone out alone on this particular date. It was an anniversary but not one to celebrate. It was the anniversary of his wife's and daughter's deaths. He considered himself to be neither an emotional nor sentimental man. No, he chose to remember what had happened to Katerina and Sofia because their sad fate was *his* worst-ever failure. His ferocious anger, injured pride and bitterness had led to that ultimate tragedy, which could not, in conscience, ever be forgotten. Out of respect for the family he had lost, he chose to remember them one wretched day a year and wallow in his shamed self-loathing. It was little enough, and it chastened him, kept him grounded, he acknowledged grimly. After all, he had screwed up, he had screwed up *so* badly that it had cost two human lives that could have been saved had he only been a more forgiving and compassionate man.

Tragically, the traits of compassion and forgiveness had never run strong in Alastor, known as Tor, Sarantos. Although he came from a kind and loving family, he was tough, inflexible and fierce in nature as befitted a billionaire banker, celebrated for his ruthless reputation, financial acumen and foresight, his advice as much sought by governments as by rich private investors. In business, he was a very high flyer. In his private life, he was appallingly aware that he had proved to be a loser. However, that was a secret he was determined to take to his grave with him, as was the truth that he would never remarry.

That was why he rarely went home now to his family in Greece. Not only did he have an understandable wish to avoid meetings with his Italian half-brother, Sevastiano, but he also didn't want to listen to his relatives talking with increasingly evangelical fervour about him 'moving on'. On his visits, a parade of suitable young women was served up at parties and dinners even though he had done everything possible to make it brutally obvious that he had no desire to find another wife and settle down again.

After all, he had long since transformed from the young man happily wed to his first love into a womaniser known throughout Europe for his passionate but short-lived affairs. At twenty-eight, he was generations removed from the naïve and idealistic man he had once been, but his family stubbornly refused to accept the change in him. Of course, his parents were as much in love now as they had been on the day of their marriage and fully believed that that happiness was achievable by all. Tor didn't plan to be the party pooper who told them that lies, deceit and betrayal had flourished, unseen and unsuspected, within their own family circle. He preferred to let his relatives live in their sunny version of reality where rainbows and unicorns flourished. He had learned the hard way that, once lost, trust and innocence were irretrievable.

Dressing for his night out, Tor set aside his gold cufflinks, his platinum watch, all visible signs of his wealth, and chose the anonymity of faded designer jeans and a leather jacket. He would go to a bar alone and drink himself almost insensible while he pondered the past and then he would climb into a taxi and come home. That was all he did. Allowing himself to forget, allowing himself to truly move on, would be, he honestly believed, an unmerited release from the guilt he deserved to suffer.

Eighteen months later

Tor frowned as his housekeeper appeared in his home office doorway, looking unusually flustered. 'Something wrong?'

'Someone's abandoned a baby on the doorstep, sir,' Mrs James informed him uncomfortably. 'A little boy about nine months old.'

'A…*baby*?' Tor stressed in astonishment.

'Security are about to check the video surveillance tapes,' the older woman told him before stiffly moving forward. 'There was a note. It's addressed to you, sir.'

'Me?' Tor said in disbelief as an envelope was slid onto his desk.

There was his name, block printed in black felt-tip pen.

'Do you want me to call the police?'

Tor was tearing open the envelope as the question was asked. The message within was brief.

This is your child.
Look after it.

Obviously, it couldn't possibly be *his* child. But what if it belonged to one of his family? He had three younger brothers, all of whom had enjoyed stays at his London town house within recent memory. What if the child should prove to be a nephew or niece? Clearly, the mother must have been desperate for help when she chose to abandon the baby and run.

'The police?' Mrs James prompted.

'No. We won't call them...yet,' Tor hedged, thinking that if one of his family was involved, he did not want a scandal or media coverage of any kind erupting from an indiscreet handling of the situation. 'I'll look into this first.'

'So, what do I do with it?'

'With what?'

'The baby, sir,' the housekeeper extended drily. 'I've no experience with young children.'

His fine ebony brows pleated. 'Contact a nanny agency for emergency cover,' he advised. 'In the meantime, I'll sort this out.'

A baby? Of course, it couldn't be his! Logic stirred, reminding him that no form of contraception was deemed entirely foolproof. Accidents happened. For that matter, *deliberate* accidents could also occur if a woman chose to be manipulative.

Like other men, he had heard stories of pins stuck in condoms to damage them and other such distasteful ruses, but he had never actually met anyone whom it had happened to.

Fake horror stories, he told himself bracingly.

Yet, momentarily, unease still rippled through Tor, connected with the unfortunate memory of the strange hysterical girl who had stormed his office the year before...

Eighteen months earlier

Pixie used the key to let herself into the plush house that was her temporary home. Several glamorous, high-earning individuals shared the dwelling, and as a poor and ordinary student nurse she was fully conscious that she was enjoying a luxury treat in staying there. She was happy with that, simply grateful to be enjoying a two-week escape from living under the same roof with her brother and his partner, who, sadly, seemed to be in the process of breaking up.

Listening to Jordan and Eloise constantly fighting, when there was absolutely no privacy, had become seriously embarrassing in the small terraced home she shared with them.

For that reason, it had been a total joy to learn that Steph, the sister of one of her friends, had a precious Siamese kitten, which she didn't want to abandon to a boarding facility while she was abroad on a modelling assignment. Initially, Pixie had been surprised that Steph didn't expect her housemates to look after her pet. Only after moving in to look after Coco had she understood that it was a house-

hold where the tenants all operated as independent
entities, coming and going without interest in their
housemates in a totally casual way that had con-
founded Pixie's rosy expectations of communal life
with her peers.

But in the short term, Pixie reminded herself,
she was enjoying the huge indulgence of a private
bathroom and a large bedroom with the sole responsibility of caring for a very cute kitten. As she was
currently working twelve-hour shifts on her annual
placement for her final year of nursing training, living in the elegant town house was a treat and she
was grateful for the opportunity. A long bath, she
promised herself soothingly as she stepped into the
room and Coco jumped onto her feet, desperate for
some attention after a day spent alone.

In auto mode, Pixie ran a bath, struggling greatly
not to dwell on the reality that during her shift in
A & E she had had to deal with her first death as
a nurse. It had been a young, healthy woman, not
something any amount of training could have prepared her for, she acknowledged ruefully. Put it in
a box at the back of her brain, she instructed herself irritably. It was not her role to get all *personally* emotional, it was her job to be supportive and
to deal with the practical and the grieving relatives
with all the tact and empathy she could summon up.

Well, she was satisfied that she had done her
job to the best of her ability, but the wounding re-

ality of that tragic passing was still lingering with her. She was not supposed to bring her work or the inevitable fatalities she would see home with her, she reminded herself doggedly, striving to live up to the professional nursing standards she admired. But at twenty-one, still scarred as she was by her own family bereavement six years earlier, it was a tough struggle to take death in her stride as a daily occurrence.

Dressed in comfy shorty pyjamas and in bare feet because the house was silent and seemingly empty, it being too early in the evening for the partying tenants to be home while others were travelling for work or pleasure. At this time of day and in the very early morning, Pixie usually had the place to herself, her antisocial working hours often a plus. She lit only the trendy lamp hanging over the kitchen island, hopelessly thrilled with the magazine perfection of her surroundings. Moulded work surfaces, fancy units and a sunroom extension leading out into a front courtyard greeted her appreciative gaze. Pixie loved to daydream and sometimes she allowed herself to dream that this was *her* house and she was cooking for the special man in her life. Special man, that was a joke, she thought ruefully, wincing away even from the dim reflection she caught of herself in the patio doors, a short curvy figure with a shock of green hair.

Green! What had possessed her when she had

dyed her hair a few weeks earlier? Her brother Jordan's lively and outspoken partner, Eloise, had persuaded her into the change at a moment when Pixie was feeling low because the man she was attracted to had yet to even notice that she was alive. Antony was a paramedic, warm and friendly, exactly the sort of man Pixie thought would be her perfect match.

But the hair had been a very bad idea, particularly when the cheap dye had refused to wash out as it was supposed to have done and she had then checked the instructions to belatedly discover that the lotion wasn't recommended for blond hair. She had hated her blond curls from the instant she was christened 'Poodle' at school, and not by her enemies but by her supposed friends. In recent weeks, she had learned that green curls were far worse than blond because everyone, from her nursing mentor to her superiors and work colleagues, had let her know that green hair in a professional capacity was a mistake. And she couldn't afford to go to a hairdresser for help. She might be working a placement, but it was unpaid, and because of her twelve-hour shifts it was virtually impossible for her to maintain a part-time job as well.

Still preoccupied with her worries, Pixie dragged out her toasted sandwich machine and put the ingredients together for a cheese toastie. It was literally all she could afford for a main meal. In fact, Coco the cat ate much better than she did. She put on the kettle, thought she heard a sound somewhere close by and blamed it on the cat she had left playing with a rubber ball in her room next door. Coco was lively but, like most kittens, she tired quickly and would fold up in a heap in her little princess fur-lined basket long before Pixie got to sleep.

While she waited for her toastie, Pixie contemplated the reality that she was returning to her brother's house that weekend. She hated living as a third wheel in Jordan's relationship with Eloise, but she didn't have much choice and, since he had lost his job over an unfortunate expenses claim that his employers had regrettably deemed a fraud rather than a mistake, Jordan was having a rough time. All his rows with Eloise were over money because he hadn't found work since he had been sacked and naturally, the bills were mounting up, which in turn made Pixie feel terrible because she was only an added burden in her brother's currently challenging existence.

Jordan had become her guardian when their parents died unexpectedly when she was fifteen and he was twenty-three. Pixie was painfully aware that Jordan could have washed his hands of her and let her go into foster care, particularly when they were, strictly speaking, only half-siblings, having been born from the same father but to different mothers, her father having been married and widowed before he met her mother. Even so, Jordan hadn't turned his back on her as he could have done. He'd had to jump through a lot of hoops to satisfy the authorities that he would be an acceptable guardian for an adolescent girl. She owed Jordan a lot for the care and support he had unstintingly given her over the years, seeing her through her school years and then her nursing course.

'Something smells good…'

At the sound of an unfamiliar male voice, Pixie almost leapt a foot in the air, her head swivelling with a jerk to focus on the strange man slowly spinning round the recliner in the unlit sunroom, where he had apparently been seated unnoticed by her.

'Heaven must be missing an angel' was the cheesiest pickup approach Pixie had ever received, but for the very first time she was looking at a man who might legitimately have inspired such a line with his sleek dark fallen-angel beauty. He *was* otherworldly in his sheer masculine perfection. Her heart was still beating very fast with fright and, striving to crush those inappropriate thoughts, she stepped forward. She collided involuntarily with the eyes of an apex predator—sharp, shrewd, powerful and dark as the night sky. 'I didn't see you in there… who are you?' she asked as civilly as she could, fearful of causing offence to any of Steph's housemates or their friends.

'I'm Tor,' he murmured. 'I think I must have fallen asleep before I called a taxi to take me home.'

'I didn't know anyone was here. I've just come in from work and I was making some supper,' Pixie confided. 'Who are you visiting here?'

His brow furrowed. Slowly, he sank back down on the recliner. 'My apologies... I don't recall her name. A leggy redhead with an annoying giggle.'

'Saffron,' Pixie told him with concealed amusement. 'But why did she just leave you in here?'

He shrugged. 'She stormed off. I rejected her and it made her angry.'

'You rejected...*Saffron*?' Pixie queried in disbelief because Saffron, a wannabe actress, resembled a supermodel and turned heads in the street.

'A misunderstanding,' he corrected smoothly. 'I thought I was coming to a party. She thought something else. I'm sorry. I'm rather drunk, not in proper control of my tongue.'

No way was he drunk!

Pixie was accustomed to dealing with surly drunks at A & E and usually they could barely vocalise or stand without swaying or cursing. He was speaking with perfect diction and courtesy and remained astute enough to smooth over the unfortunate impression he might have made in saying bluntly that he had rejected the other woman. All the same, she hadn't thought there was a man born who wouldn't jump at the chance of having sex with the gorgeous redhead. Presumably, Saffron had either sought the privacy of her own room upstairs to handle such a blow to her ego or she had gone out again, but Pixie could only be impressed by a man particular enough in his tastes to say no to a beauty like Saffron.

'What are you cooking?' he shot at her unexpectedly.

'A cheese toastie,' Pixie responded in an undertone as she lifted the lid, waved away the steam and reached for her plate.

'It smells incredible...'

'Would you like one?' she heard herself ask and she wanted to slap herself for being so impressionable.

He was a complete stranger and she owed him nothing but, as her brother's partner had warned her, she was a 'nurturer', the sort of woman whom men, according to Eloise, would take advantage of. And Pixie had seen the evidence for that condemnation in her own nature. She *did* like to feed people; she *did* like to take care of them. Pleasing people, tending to their needs, satisfied something in her, a something that Eloise believed she should suppress out of self-interest.

'I'd love that. I'm starving.' He smiled at her and that smile locked her knees where she stood because it was like a galaxy of golden warmth engulfing her, locking his lean bronzed features into shocking beauty, releasing a flock of butterflies low in her tummy. Stupid, stupid, *stupid*, she castigated herself with self-loathing as she reached for the bread and butter again before saying, 'Here… have this one… I'll have the next.'

As she pushed the plate with a knife and fork across the island, he tugged out one of the high stools and settled into it. She busied herself with the sandwich maker, her pale skin pink while he watched her, and she could feel the weight of his regard like a brand. Nothing she had felt in Antony's radius could compare to the thrumming level of awareness assailing her beneath the stranger's gaze.

The hair was weird, there was no other word for it, Tor was reflecting, his gaze locked to those tumbling pale green curls lying tousled on her narrow shoulders, but if a woman *could* rock green hair, she was rocking it. She had the brightest blue eyes he had ever seen, the softest, pinkest mouth, the most flawless skin, but she was so undersized he could barely see her behind the barrier of the island.

'What height are you?' he asked curiously.

Pixie cringed. 'About four ten…no tall genes in my family tree.'

'How old are you?'

'Why are you asking me that?'

'I'm in an unfamiliar house with unknown occupants. I don't want to find out that I'm keeping company with someone's child, and you don't look very old…'

'I'm twenty-one,' Pixie provided grudgingly. 'Almost a fully qualified nurse. Totally grown-up and independent.'

'Twenty-one is still very young,' Tor countered mildly.

'So, how old are you, old man?' Pixie enquired teasingly, putting down the lid on the second toastie and relaxing back against the kitchen cabinets to watch him eat. 'Coffee?'

'Black, sweet. I'm twenty-eight,' he told her.

'And married,' she noted without thought as the ring on his wedding finger glinted under the light and she switched on the coffee machine again. 'What were you doing with Saffron? Sorry, none of my business... I shouldn't have asked,' she muttered, backtracking in haste from that unintentional challenge.

'No offence taken. I'm a widower,' Tor volunteered.

Pixie turned back to him, stirring the coffee and passing it to him. 'I'm sorry for your loss.'

'It's OK,' Tor said with a stiffness she recognised, the awkwardness of someone unaccustomed to dealing openly with the topic of grief. 'It's been five years since my wife and my daughter died.'

Pixie paled. 'You lost your child as well?'

Pixie felt even more awkward, painfully aware of how she had felt earlier that evening when she had dealt with her first death at the hospital. The finality of a passing and the grieving family left behind scarred the staff as well. For a man to have lost both a wife and a child together was an enormous double blow and her heart squeezed on his behalf at the idea of such a huge loss.

Pale too beneath his bronzed skin, Tor jerked his chin down in silent confirmation.

'I'm so sorry,' she whispered.

'Nobody ever mentions it now. For them it's like it happened a hundred years ago,' he muttered with perceptible bitterness.

'Death makes people uncomfortable. They avoid discussing it often out of fear of saying the wrong thing.'

'Or as if it might be contagious,' Tor slotted in drily.

'I know… My parents passed within a week of each other and even my friends avoided me at school when I went back,' she told him with a grimace of recollection.

'A car accident?'

'No, they caught legionnaires' disease on a weekend away. They were both diabetic with compromised immune systems and they didn't go for treatment soon enough. They thought they'd caught some harmless virus and none of us knew any different.' Pixie shifted a wordless shoulder in pained acceptance. 'My father went first and Mum a day later. I was devastated. I had no idea how ill they were until it was too late.'

'Is that why you're doing nursing?'

'Partially. I wanted to know more so that I could help people when they needed it and I like doing useful, practical stuff.' Pixie sighed, a rueful smile tugging at her generous mouth. 'And to be frank, I was also the sort of child who bandaged teddy bears and tried to raise orphaned baby birds. My brother calls it a save-the-world mentality.'

'I have a brother too but we're estranged,' Tor heard himself volunteer, and wondered for the first time if that old saying about alcohol loosening the tongue could actually be true because he was gabbling like a chatterbox, which he was not and never had been. He was innately reserved, rather quiet outside working hours. Or was it *her* affecting him? Unthreatening and studiously unsexy as she was in her pale grey pyjamas adorned with little pink flamingos? And no sooner had he thought that than he had to notice the stupendously sexy thrust and sway of a pair of firm full breasts beneath her top as she clambered up on the stool to eat her toastie.

'You're estranged?' Her big blue eyes clouded with sympathy. 'That's sad.'

'No, it's not. He *slept* with my wife!' Tor bit out, shocking himself with that revelation, which had never crossed his lips before, not to anyone, not for any reason, a sordid secret he had planned to keep buried until the day he died.

Pixie's eyes widened in shock. 'Oh, my goodness…' she gasped. 'Your brother did *that*?'

'He and I didn't grow up together. We are not close,' Tor acknowledged grudgingly. 'But I could never forgive him for that betrayal.'

'Of course, you couldn't.'

That first confession having leapt from his tongue, Tor was discovering that for some inexplicable reason he could not hold back the rest. 'On the night my wife died she admitted that she had fallen in love with Sev *before* we married but that she fought her feelings out of loyalty to me and assumed she would get over him.'

'She still shouldn't have married you,' Pixie opined feelingly. 'She should've told you she was having doubts before the wedding.'

'That would certainly have been less devastating than the end result.' His lean, bronzed face could have been sculpted out of granite, his dark-as-night eyes flinty and hard. 'Finding out several years down the road that our whole life together was a fake, a *lie*, was much worse and…and I didn't handle it well,' he completed in a raw undertone.

'I should think you were in shock.' Pixie sighed, retrieving his coffee mug and moving to refill it.

'Still doesn't excuse me.' The eyes she had believed were so dark focused on her absently and she saw the gleams of gold lightening them to bronze. Such beautiful eyes, fringed and enhanced by ridiculously long black lashes. He was shockingly attractive, she thought, struggling to concentrate and avert her attention from the perfect slash of his dark brows, the exotic slant of his high cheekbones and the fullness of his mouth.

'Why? What did you do?' she prompted.

'When I arrived home, she was putting cases into her car. That was when she told me about the affair…at the very last minute. I had no suspicion that there was another man in her life but, after three years of what I had believed was a happy marriage, she was just going to leave me a note.' His nostrils flared with disgust. 'We had a massive argument. It was…chaotic,' he selected roughly. 'I barely knew what I was saying.'

'Shock,' she told him again. 'It intensifies everything you feel but at the same time you're not yourself. You're not in control.'

'I said a great deal I regret… I was cruel,' Tor admitted unevenly, biting back the final shameful admission that Katerina had made, which had torn him apart: her insistence that the daughter he loved was *not* his child but had been fathered by her lover.

'You weren't prepared. You had no time to think.'

Warmed by her compassionate need to console him, he reached for her hand where it rested on the counter and squeezed it gently before withdrawing his touch again. 'You may be able to save the world, but you can't save me from a world of regret. Katerina raced upstairs to lift our daughter out of her cot. My wife was very worked up by that stage and in no condition to drive. I tried to reason with her, but she wouldn't listen to me. Sofia was screaming and upset...'

His voice had become gruff and he lifted his hands to scrub at his face, wiping away the dampness on his cheeks, and her heart went out to him in that moment because she knew that he was recalling the guilt and powerlessness that grief inflicted. 'It was all madness that night, madness and chaos,' he continued. 'Katerina drove off far too fast and the car skidded on the icy drive and careened into a wall.'

'So, you saw it happen.' Pixie was lost for words, full of sympathy for him, able to see that he was still torturing himself for what he had said and done that night in his own shock and distress.

'And it was too late to change anything,' he completed in a curt undertone.

Her eyes connected with his, awash with fellow feeling and understanding. 'You recall every wrong thing you ever did or said to the person. Every emotion is exaggerated. When my mother was passing, I was beating myself up for being cheeky to her when she had told me to clean my room. That's being human.'

Tor sat back tautly. 'I don't know why I've told you all this. I've never talked to anyone about it before.'

'No one?' Pixie pressed in surprise.

'I didn't want to tell anyone the truth about what happened that night. I didn't want anyone judging Katerina or thinking less of her. The truth wouldn't have eased the shock of her death and my daughter's for anyone, least of all her own family. It would only have caused greater distress.'

'But staying silent, forcing yourself to go on living a lie made it harder for *you*,' Pixie slotted in with a frown.

'I've got broad shoulders...and I really don't know what I'm doing here,' Tor confessed, the smouldering, breathtaking appeal of his bemused eyes and drowsy smile washing over her, imbuing her with a sense of connection she had never felt with any man before. 'It must be true that it's easier to talk to a stranger. But I think it's time for me to order that taxi.'

'Possibly,' Pixie muttered self-consciously, scrambling off the stool in haste and beginning to tidy up to keep her hands busy. She stacked the dishwasher, darting round the island at speed to gather up the dishes before opening the tall larder cupboard to stow away the clutter of condiments that had been left sitting out.

'What's the address?' he asked her as he paced several feet away with his phone in his hand, a dep-

recatory smile of great charm curving his mobile
mouth at his having to ask that basic question that
divulged the reality that he truly didn't know where
he was.

For a split second she couldn't drag her eyes
from him, that half-smile somehow enhanced by
the black shadow of stubble framing it and defin-
ing his strong jawline, his eyes gleaming a glorious
tigerish gold. There was a condensed power to him,
a leashed energy that sprang out at her.

Pixie had to think for a second before trotting
out the address in a rush, stumbling and correct-
ing herself with the number, and she was already
scolding herself for her reaction to him. He was a
very, *very* good-looking guy and naturally she had
noticed, but she had also immediately recognised
that he was way, way out of her league. She was
ordinary, he was something far superior, not only
in the looks department, but also with his instinc-
tive assurance and ingrained courtesy.

'The taxi will be here in five minutes.' Tor dug the
phone back into his jeans and walked towards her.

'I'll wait outside. Thanks for feeding me…and
for listening,' he murmured ruefully. 'I didn't even
ask you for your name.'

She laughed. 'Pixie…'

His brows pleated as he stared at her. *'Pixie?'*

'I was a very small, premature baby. Mum

thought it was cute.' Pixie wrinkled her tip-tilted nose, eyes blue as cornflowers gazing up at him.

Marvelling at the truth that she was barely tall enough to reach his chest, for he stood over six feet in height, he extended a lean brown hand. 'I'm Alastor Sarantos but I've always been called Tor.'

'Pleased to meet you.'

As he swung away to leave, he walked head first into the larder cupboard door and reeled back from it, sufficiently stunned by the blow to his temple to grab the edge of the island to steady himself and stay upright. Pixie gasped and rushed over to him.

'No…no, stay still, don't move,' she warned him. 'You hit your head hard.'

His hand lifted to his temple in a clumsy motion and he blinked in bemusement. 'That hurt,' he admitted.

Guilt assailed Pixie as she glimpsed the still-swinging door, which she had neglected to close. It was her fault that he had been injured. 'Can I check your head?' she asked.

'I'm fine,' he told her, even as he swayed, and he frowned at her because, she reckoned, he was having difficulty focusing on her.

'No, you're not. Nobody could be fine after smacking their head that hard,' she declared, running light fingers across his temple, feeling the bump in dismay while being relieved that he hadn't cut himself and there was no blood. 'You're not bleeding but you are going to have a huge bruise. I think you should have it checked out at A & E because you probably have a concussion.'

'I will be absolutely fine.' Tor swore impatiently as he attempted to walk away and staggered slightly.

'You're still very dizzy. Take a moment to get steady. You can lie down in my room until the taxi arrives,' Pixie murmured as she planted a bracing arm to his spine and directed him down the hall to the room next door. He towered over her, his big powerful frame rigid as he attempted to put mind over matter.

'Are you feeling sick?'

'No,' he told her very drily.

No, big masculine men didn't like to be knocked off balance by any form of weakness, she thought, feeling guiltier than ever about his plight and his doubtless aching head as she pushed open the door of her room and guided him over to the bed.

He lowered himself down and kicked off his shoes. Pixie set them side by side neatly on the rug. 'You can nap. You seem to be thinking coherently.'

From his prone position, Tor rested dazed, long-suffering dark golden eyes on her anxious face. 'I don't want to be saved right now. Go save someone else,' he urged.

It was a polite way of telling her that she was being irritating and she gritted her teeth on a sharp comeback.

CHAPTER TWO

'WHY GREEN?' Tor mumbled.

'The hair?' Embarrassed, Pixie touched a hand to her hair and grimaced. 'I wanted to be different.'

'It's different,' Tor confirmed, wondering when he had last seen a woman blush, and it looked like an all-over blush too, a slow tide of colour sweeping up from her throat to her hairline.

Pixie winced. 'There was a guy I was hoping would notice me at work. *And* he did notice,' she admitted with a slight grimace. 'Antony said I reminded him of a leprechaun.'

A spontaneous laugh broke from Tor. 'Not quite the effect you were looking for? I shouldn't tease you. *Diavole...* I am drunk,' he groaned, watching the ceiling revolve for his benefit. 'Where's my taxi got to?'

'It should be here soon,' she said soothingly. 'Just chill.'

'Don't have a lot of practice at just chilling. I'm naturally impatient.'

Pixie sat on her knees by the bed because there was nowhere else to sit in the room. She breathed in deep and slow. She was very tired but she had to stay awake until the taxi arrived and she saw him off. At least he had taken her mind off what had happened during her shift: the pointless death of a young life in a car accident, a young woman on the brink of marriage, deeply mourned by her heartbroken fiancé and her devastated family.

'What's he like? The guy you want to notice you?' Tor prompted without warning, startling her out of her reverie.

'What's it matter? Leprechauns aren't sexy,' she pointed out in a defeatist tone. 'Antony's a paramedic so I don't know much about him, only that he's a lovely guy. For all I know, he could have a girlfriend.'

'I think you look more like a forest fairy than a leprechaun,' Tor remarked, wondering when a woman had last told him that she was attracted to someone else rather than him. He didn't think it had *ever* happened to him. It was a startling, disconcerting novelty. He was used to walking into a bar and every beautiful woman there making a beeline for him. He was young, he was rich, he was single. That was how his world worked and casual sex was always easily available, not something he had to plan.

Before his marriage, though, he hadn't had much experience. He had grown up with Katerina. Their families had been and still were friends. He had known even as a teenager that he would marry Katerina and he had insisted on going ahead and marrying her when he was only twenty. Maybe his parents had been right when they had tried to talk him out of that, tried to tell him that they were too young. He had been ready for that commitment but evidently Katerina hadn't been. Yet he had honestly believed that she loved him the way he loved her.

Forest fairy? That sounded rather more complimentary than a leprechaun, Pixie was reflecting ruefully. OK, she was fishing for hope! What he had already taught her without even trying was that what she had regarded as attraction with Antony was a laughable shadow in comparison to the way in which Tor drew her. Perhaps she had only focused on Antony because there was nobody else around and she had yet to find a boyfriend.

'Maybe that depends on your point of view. If I still look like I belong in a kid's storybook, it's not exactly seductive,' Pixie muttered. 'But you've definitely got the gift of the gab.'

'Gift of the gab? What's that?' he questioned.

'A ready tongue. You know the right thing to say. If you were interested in a woman, you would know better than to compare her to a leprechaun,' she guessed.

'That's true,' Tor acknowledged without hesitation.

Pixie studied him, liking his honesty in admitting that, where women were involved, he was as smooth and cutting edge as glass, instinctively knowing the right words to impress and please. That fitted. No guy as downright gorgeous as he was could be an innocent or clumsy with his words. He had already been married, which made her respect and trust him more because he had committed to *one* woman young when he must have had so many other options.

In his marriage, however, he had been badly burned, she reflected with fierce compassion, because the woman he had married had betrayed his trust and *hurt* him. And that was what he was *truly* struggling with, she decided thoughtfully. He wasn't only striving to handle the pain of loss, but he was also dealing with the pain of being betrayed by someone whom he had loved and trusted.

She went out to the front door to check for any sign of the taxi, but the street was quiet. She padded back into her room, colliding with watchful dark eyes shot through with accents of gold. He really did have the most beautiful eyes and the thickest, longest, blackest lashes and any woman would have noticed those attractions, she reasoned uncomfortably. The guy had dynamite sex appeal. 'Why were you on your own tonight?' she asked him curiously as she leant over him.

'I go out every year on this date and remember

Katerina's and Sofia's deaths,' he confided, dismaying her.

'If you have to drink to handle those memories, it's a destructive habit,' Pixie told him gently. 'It would be wiser to talk about them and leave the booze out of it.'

Tor pushed himself up on his elbows. 'And what would you know about it?'

'I lost my parents six years ago,' she reminded him. 'I used my nursing course to work through those feelings of loss by helping other people. I have to deal with bereaved people at work on a regular basis. Sometimes their unhappiness makes me feel anxious and sad. Let me look at your head.'

She had the brightest blue eyes and a full soft pink mouth. Arousal slithered through Tor and he struggled to master it and concentrate on the conversation as he lowered his head. 'And how do you handle it?'

'I have a box with a lid at the back of my mind. At work I cram anything that makes me uncomfortable in there and then close the lid down tight. I don't allow myself to think about any of it until the end of my shift.'

He shivered as gentle fingertips brushed his brow and delicately traced the bump. He was already imagining those soft fingers smoothing over a far more sensitive part of his body and he castigated himself for his arousal because she had been kind to him and she was too young for him, possibly not that experienced either. She didn't deserve for him to take advantage of her sympathetic nature.

'All that restraint sounds rather too taxing for me.' Tor tilted his head back again to look up at her.

And her heartbeat pounded like a crazed drum as their eyes met again, a wild fluttering breaking free in her tummy even as an almost painful ache thrummed between her thighs. It was lust, instant and raw and nothing at all like the simple sexual curiosity Antony had stirred in her. A man had never made her feel anything that powerful before and that shocking intensity stopped her dead in her tracks. Long brown fingers reached up to lace with care into her curls, tugging her head down to his.

'I want to kiss you,' Tor murmured almost fiercely.

'Do it,' she heard herself urge without hesitation, so greedy was she for more of the new sensations he had awakened.

And his mouth tasted hers, gently parting and seeking, startling her with that sensual testing appeal and warm invitation. His mouth sent a curling flame of liquid heat to the heart of her, which made her lean down, instinctively seeking more of the same. Long, lazy arms extending, he brought her down on top of him and effortlessly turned them both over, flipping her down onto the bed beside him without her registering any sense of alarm.

In fact, as he slid partially over her, the weight

of one masculine leg parting hers, a naked thrill of
excitement raced through Pixie and her entire body
tingled as the tip of his tongue skidded over the roof
of her mouth. Nothing had ever felt so good or so
necessary as the hot urgency of his mouth on hers.
She was no innocent when it came to kissing but
never before had she enjoyed kisses that set her on
fire. Beneath her top she was ridiculously conscious
of the heavy swell of her breasts and the prickling
tightening of her nipples while in her pelvis a com-
bustible mix of heat and craving seethed.

He eased a hand below her top and cupped her
breast, his thumb rubbing an urgently tender nipple, and her back arched and her hips bucked, and a
breathless moan was torn from her lips without her
volition. He thrust the top out of his path and locked
his mouth to the straining, tightly beaded tip of her
nipple and her whole body rose against his on the
surge of tormenting sensation that darted straight
to the hollow between her legs.

'I love your body,' he husked. 'It's so sexy.'

And her lashes almost fluttered open on surprised eyes because she had never been told she was
sexy before. No, she was always the girl the stray
men locked on to and shared their life stories with.
They told her about their past break-ups and what
sort of girl they were hoping to meet. It was never
ever a short curvy blonde who liked to listen and
didn't like exercise much. No, it was always some-

one tall, slim and into the gym. She had more gay friends than heterosexual ones, friends who told her she needed to be more confident, outgoing and chatty if she wanted men to notice her. That instant of clear thought and surprise faded as Tor divided his attentions between her breasts with a single-minded intensity that destroyed any control she had over her sensation-starved body.

Tor was making her feel sexy. He was making her feel good about herself and her body and the burning, yearning ache at her feminine core, making her hips writhe, cutting through every other consideration she might have had. He touched her *there*, where she needed that touch most, tracing her slick folds with skilled fingertips, toying with her to make her gasp and then circling her unbearably sensitive core until she didn't know what she was doing any more, only knew that her body felt like one giant yawning scream in desperate need of release. She was shifting, moving, out of control, feverish with a need she had never felt so strongly before.

'Want me?' he groaned as he skimmed off her pyjama bottoms.

'*Yes!*' she exclaimed, longing for that gnawing hunger to be satisfied.

'*Thee mou...* I've never wanted anything the way I want you right now!' Tor growled, shifting over her, rearranging her willing body to push her legs up and back and higher.

And then he was surging into her, partially sating that desire for more with a compelling rush of new sensations. There was the burn as he stretched her tight channel and then a sudden sharp sting of pain as he plunged deeper. It made her grit her teeth but before she could linger on that development a whole host of new reactions was washing her memory of it away.

'So tight, so *good*, you feel amazing, *moraki mou*,' he framed raggedly, dark eyes sheer smouldering golden enticement as he looked down at her, shifting his lithe hips to send another cascade of sensual response travelling through her pliant body that made her breath catch on a gasp of wonder.

What had momentarily felt new and disconcertingly intense now felt absolutely right. Deep down inside, her body was tightening and tightening while his every passionate stroke inside her sent a sweet tide of rapturous sensation rippling through her. His urgency increased her breathless excitement. She thought her heart was about to burst from her chest. Only quick, shallow breaths came to her lungs and her body was rising up to his until finally the unbearable tension gripping her broke and she convulsed, her body clenching tight on his as an exquisite surge of release sent her over the edge and engulfed her in ecstasy.

In the wake of that shattering conclusion, Pixie stirred, shifting out awkwardly from beneath Tor's weight. 'Tor?' she whispered. *'Tor?'*

She scrambled out of bed, worriedly scanning him. Breathing normally, he was fast asleep. Her fingers grazed his brow, but his temperature was already cooling from his exertions on her behalf. Her face flamed hotter than hellfire.

Pixie was in shock as she eased back into her pyjama shorts with a wince because a part of her that she didn't want to think about just then was sore. Tor had kept on warning her that he was very drunk, but she hadn't really believed him. Some people retained better control under the influence of alcohol, and he was clearly one of those individuals, capable of having a normal conversation and putting up a front. His conduct, however, was more revealing, she conceded uneasily. Intoxicated people were less inhibited, more liable to succumb to impulsive, uncharacteristic behaviour.

And having sex with her could only have been a random impulse and something he wouldn't have done under any other circumstances. She could feel the blood draining from her shaken face as she made that deduction.

Saffron had brought him home for sex and he had said no. While respectfully engaged in remembering the death of his loved ones, Tor had not wanted a one-night stand with anyone. Pixie completely un-

derstood that, so she could not explain how she had
lost control of the situation to the extent of actually
having sex with Tor. How had that happened? How
had she contrived to take advantage of a guy who
was drunk and probably concussed and confused
into the bargain?

She hurried into the compact en suite bathroom
and went for a quick shower, registering in consternation as she undressed that neither one of them
had thought to use contraception. She lifted chilled
hands to her distraught face because she wasn't on
the birth-control pill or the shot or anything, having deemed such advance precautions unnecessary
when she had yet to have even a relationship with
a man and had never felt any urge to try more casual encounters.

Of course, she could ask for the morning-after
pill, she reminded herself, and tensed at the prospect of having to make that decision. Why was that
the exact moment when she had to recall her late
mother tugging her curls and saying, 'You were
my little surprise baby!' Although she hadn't been
planned by her parents, both of whom had been in
their forties when she was unexpectedly conceived,
she had been welcomed into the world and loved all
the same. How could she do any less for any child
she conceived?

Well, she *was* being a little theatrical in imagining such a challenging scenario in the immedi-

ate aftermath of her *first* sexual encounter, she told herself in exasperation.

But in truth, she was in shock at what she had done. She wasn't an impulsive person and yet from that first scorching kiss she had succumbed to Tor and had encouraged his every move. She hadn't made the smallest attempt to call a halt, she reminded herself crushingly. Her body and the fiery seduction of her own eager responses had enthralled her. All these years, it seemed, she had totally underestimated the fact that sexual arousal genuinely could lead to seriously bad choices.

Tor was gorgeous and he had got her all excited and everything that had happened from that point had been *her* fault. He had told her that he was drunk, and she had seen for herself that he was probably concussed. She had chosen to have sex with a drunk, grieving man and could only thank herself for the powerful sense of humiliation and shame that she was now enduring. *She* had taken advantage of *him*.

Pixie moved back into the bedroom, where Tor still slept. In only a couple of hours she had to get up again and go to work. She got back on the bed and clung to her side of it, eyes so heavy they ached. She felt sad, ashamed that she had been so foolish as to get carried away like a wayward teenager with the excitement of sex. She knew better, she knew the risks to her health and happiness and knew she would be visiting a clinic as soon as possible to be checked and go on some form of birth control. Although the guilt currently assailing her warned that she was highly unlikely to make such a mistake twice.

His phone was buzzing in his pocket and she drew it out with careful fingers and gently switched it off before replacing it. She was in no mood to be confronted by an angry, confused man because she couldn't explain what had happened between them either.

Dawn was lightening the skies when she rose again and quietly dressed for her shift. Tor was still heavily asleep, and she decided to leave him to let himself out. That approach would neatly sidestep any embarrassing conversations or partings. She never ever wanted to lay eyes on the guy again!

CHAPTER THREE

TEARS WERE BURNING the backs of Pixie's eyes as she sat stiffly in the waiting area of the opulent office building. The receptionist was exasperated with her for refusing to take a polite hint and leave: Tor Sarantos was not available for an appointment or even a phone conversation with anyone whose name wasn't on the 'approved' list.

So, how was she supposed to tell the man that he had got her pregnant? Putting such a confidential disclosure in a letter struck her as foolish and careless. It would be read by office staff and likely discarded as the ravings of some desperate wannabe striving to importune the boss. And if it *was* given to him, he would be embarrassed that employees had been made aware of information that he would probably prefer stayed private.

Yes, Tor Sarantos, banker extraordinaire, had certainly been hiding his light under a bushel, a virtual forest of bushels, according to everything that

Pixie had learned about him on the internet and in the media in the months since their meeting. He was an incredibly rich and important banker and as far removed from her ordinary world as a gold nugget would be in a wastepaper bin. Only the craziest accident of fate could have ever let them meet in the first place, never mind conceive a child together.

It had taken Pixie quite a few months to decide that she *had* to tell Tor that she was pregnant. It was his right to know that he was going to be a father again. She would never forget the devastation she had seen in his haunted eyes when he told her about his wife and daughter dying. He had loved and cared for his daughter and it was that fact more than any other that had forced Pixie to listen to her conscience and seek him out.

He might not want any sort of relationship with her, but he might well want a relationship with their child, and she could not bring herself to deny either him or their unborn child that opportunity.

She was almost six months pregnant now. And, so far, pregnancy was proving to be a long, exhausting haul. She had finished her nursing training before she even allowed herself to acknowledge her symptoms and do a pregnancy test. She had wasted weeks running away from a looming truth that frightened her, she acknowledged shamefacedly, afraid to face the trial of being pregnant, alone and unsupported.

Her brother had been incredulous. 'You're a nurse!' he had exclaimed when she had told him. 'How could someone with your training fall pregnant? Why weren't you on birth control? And why haven't you gone for a termination yet?'

Yes, there had been loads of awkward, painful conversations between her sibling and her, conversations mostly bereft of Eloise's more sympathetic input because her brother and his partner had split up and Eloise had moved out. Sadly too, although Pixie still saw Eloise as a friend away from the house, Eloise's departure had worsened their financial situation and made meeting the mortgage payments an even bigger challenge.

Thankfully, however, Pixie was now able to work and contribute to the household bills, but the larger she got, the harder she was finding it to work a twelve-hour shift. Her exhaustion had been another factor that had persuaded her that she needed help and that she had to approach Tor for it even if it was the very last thing she wanted to do.

After all, it wasn't as though she had even been a one-night stand who had fallen inconveniently pregnant. Tor hadn't sought her out, hadn't personally selected her from any crowd of available women, he had simply kissed her and ended up having sex with her because he had fallen asleep in the wrong kitchen. Proximity had been their downfall and every step of the way she had encouraged

him with her willingness. She should have said no,
she should have called a halt but, controlled by that
crazy excitement, she had been greedy, immature
and selfish.

Pixie was still convinced that Tor would not have
chosen to have sex with her had he been in full control of himself. But alcohol, grief and a nasty blow
to the head had made him vulnerable and she, who
should have known better, had urged him on.

Even worse, she didn't want to be another problem in his life. She didn't want to upset him. But
once she'd realised that false pride was keeping her
from reaching out for the assistance she needed, she
had finally seen common sense. Unhappily, getting
a personal meeting with Tor was probably as easy
as getting to have tea with the Queen.

'Miss Miller, I've called Security to show you
the way out,' the receptionist informed her with a
fixed, unnatural smile. 'There's no point in you sitting here waiting when Mr Sarantos is unavailable.'

And that was when Pixie appreciated that by following the rules she had got as close to Tor as she
was ever likely to get. As soon as the receptionist
returned to her desk, Pixie rose and began walking down the wide corridor that led to the imposing double doors, behind which she had estimated
lay Tor's office.

A shout hastened her steps. 'Hey! You can't go

in there! Security… *Security!*' The receptionist was screeching at the top of her voice.

Pixie thrust down the door handle and stalked right in. Tor swung round with a phone gripped in one hand. Impossibly elegant and tall, he wore a dark pinstriped suit teamed with a white shirt and a snazzy red tie. He looked indescribably sophisticated and intimidating, not remotely like the man who had sat at the kitchen island and eaten a cheese toasted sandwich with every evidence of normal enjoyment.

'What is the meaning of this interruption?' Tor demanded imperiously, studying her with frowning intensity.

And Pixie held her breath and waited…and waited…for recognition to colour that cool, distant stare. It didn't happen, and that absence of recognition flustered her even more.

'Don't you remember me, Tor?' she murmured almost pleadingly, cringing inwardly from that note in her own voice.

'I don't know who you are. How could I remember you?' he enquired cuttingly, his attention lowering to the prominent swell of her abdomen, his wide sensual mouth tightening when he registered that she was pregnant.

'That night you were with me last year,' she whispered uncertainly, tears involuntarily stinging her eyes at having to voice that lowering reminder. 'I came to tell you that I'm pregnant.'

Derision hardened his lean, darkly handsome features. 'I've never seen you before and if you want to make fanciful allegations of that nature, I suggest you approach my lawyers in the usual fashion.'

'Sorry about this, sir. She wouldn't listen to reason!' the receptionist snapped, a hand closing over Pixie's forearm to prevent her from moving deeper into the office. 'Security are on their way.'

Pixie had never felt so humiliated in her life.

I don't know who you are… I've never seen you before.

Perhaps it had been naïve of her not to expect that sort of rejection. Perhaps it had been ridiculously optimistic, even vain, for her to expect Tor Santos to remember her after a casual sexual encounter. To be strictly fair though, she supposed her appearance had changed since her green hair had faded and eventually washed out entirely.

Even so, she just hadn't been prepared for him to look through her as if she didn't exist, and then perceptibly wince when the tears her pregnancy hormones couldn't hold back flooded down her cheeks and a noisy sob was wrenched from her.

An older man began easing her back out of the office again and by then she was crying so hard, she could hardly see to walk. And what a terrible irony it was for her to hear Tor intervene loudly with the words, 'Be careful with her…she's pregnant!' As if he were the only person who might have noticed the vast swell of her once-flat stomach.

'Well?' Jordan had demanded expectantly, when he'd come home from his barista job that evening. 'What did he say?'

And for the first time she had told her brother a little more of the truth of how very fleeting her intimacy with Tor had been. Jordan had simply shrugged and said that such facts were irrelevant and that the father of her child still had obligations to meet.

'Not until the baby is born,' Pixie had protested, cutting through Jordan's insistence that she needed a solicitor to fight for her rights.

Jordan generally got aggressive and argumentative in difficult situations but that wasn't Pixie's way. It took her weeks to get over that distressing encounter in Tor's office, when he had denied all knowledge of her. She had wondered if Tor was telling the truth, or if indeed he remembered her perfectly well but just didn't want to be bothered or embarrassed or reminded of what had happened between them that night. And that wounding suspicion had cut her to the quick.

Admittedly, she wasn't a beauty like the women she had seen him with in the media. She wasn't a socialite, a model or an actress who swanned around in designer clothing and posed for photos. She was a very ordinary young woman. A handful of small, unexpected events and coincidences had put her on intimate terms with Tor and resulted in her ending up in bed with him.

He had been special to her, but she hadn't been special to him. They had both walked away afterwards, both of them probably feeling the same: that it shouldn't have happened. So, it didn't really matter whether Tor genuinely didn't remember her, she told herself, or whether he was simply *pretending* not to remember her. At the end of it, his distaste and derision that day in his office stayed with her and understandably coloured her attitude to him. After that experience, she was pretty convinced that even though she was pregnant by him, Tor would prefer *not* to know. and her conscience quietened. She decided that she didn't need his help and that she didn't want his financial assistance either, no matter what arguments her aggrieved brother put up!

Present day

Pixie wakened and revelled in the quietness of the house, smothering a yawn as she sat up and wondered if Jordan had taken Alfie out to the park.

She smiled as she thought of her son. He was nine months old, big and strong for his age, hitting every developmental target ahead of time and already trying to walk.

Coco slunk up the stairs to greet her with delighted purrs and she petted the cat with a warm smile. Steph had begun leaving Coco with Pixie whenever she went abroad, and weeks would pass before she finally reappeared to collect the little animal again. In the end, she had asked if Pixie would like to keep the Siamese because she was finding pet ownership too much of a tie.

Pixie crossed the landing to the bathroom and went for a quick shower before dressing. Everything she did was done by rote because she had been working night shifts since Alfie was born. In the morning she came home, fed and dressed her son and then went immediately to bed while Jordan took charge of Alfie for a few hours.

Working nights as a nurse, combined with Jordan's freedom to choose his shifts as a barista, meant that she didn't have to pay for childcare. Considering the amount of debt that her brother seemed to have acquired since he had lost his insurance job, that was fortunate. Clad in cropped jeans and a long-sleeved cotton top in raspberry pink and white stripes, she descended the creaking narrow staircase.

The terraced house was small, but she had managed to squeeze a cot into her bedroom and there was a little backyard she was currently cleaning up to serve as a play area for Alfie once he became more mobile. She was taken aback to find her brother sitting at the tiny breakfast bar with a beer.

'Where's Alfie?' she asked. 'And why are you drinking at this time of day?'

Jordan shot her a defiant look. 'I've sorted things out for you,' he said, compressing his lips.

As she took after her mother in looks, Jordan took after their father. He was tall with dark hair and a beard and spectacles, which gave him a slightly nerdy look.

'What things?' she questioned with a frown as she glanced into the cramped lounge, expecting to see her son playing on the floor with his toys. The room, however, was empty and the toy box sat untouched by the wall.

'Your situation, the mess you made having that child…against *all* my advice!' her brother complained loudly.

'Jordan…where's Alfie?' Pixie exclaimed, cutting across his words.

And then he told her, and she couldn't believe her ears, was already snatching up her coat and her bag in sheer panic at the danger he had put her son in. 'Were you out of your mind?' she demanded in disbelief.

'Alfie's his kid. *He* should be looking after him and taking care of all his needs!' Jordan countered heatedly.

'You abandoned my son in the street, where any-thing could have happened to him?' Pixie yelled at him full blast.

'No, I stood out of sight and watched to see that he was taken into the house before I walked away. I'm not an idiot and he *is* my nephew. He may be a nuisance, but I do care about the little tyke!'

'What house?' she demanded in sudden sincere bewilderment.

There was another wildly frustrating hiatus while Jordan explained how he had paid some man he met in a pub to find out Tor's London address. By the time she'd dug that information out of her sibling she'd already ordered a taxi—because no way, no how, when her baby boy was in danger, was she heading out on a bus or a train to reclaim him!

Jordan pursued her right out onto the street, heat-edly arguing his point of view, which was that her attitude towards caring for Alfie had been wrong from the start.

'You could've made a killing out of having that child and now you *will*,' Jordan declared, striking horror into her bones. 'And it'll be all thanks to me for looking out for your interests.'

'Not everything is about money, Jordan,' Pixie breathed in disgust. 'And I did *not* have Alfie to feather anyone's nest!'

She slumped in the taxi, sick to her stomach. When had money come to mean more to Jordan

than his own flesh and blood? Had she always been
blind to that side of her brother? How had she contrived to ignore the fact that Jordan had only begun
supporting her desire to have her baby *after* he had
grasped that Alfie's father was a very rich man?
Even back then, had Jordan been viewing her little
boy as a potential source of profit? As the ticket
towards an easier life? Her stomach shifted quea-
sily. And what on earth was her brother expecting
to happen now that he had confronted Tor Sarantos with the child he didn't want to know about?

Was Jordan hoping that Tor would pay handsomely for her and Alfie to go away and not bother
him again? What other scenario could he be pictur-
ing? And how could she continue living with and
entrusting Alfie's care to a man who could behave
as he had done and put an innocent child at risk?

Still in a panic, Pixie leapt out of the taxi and
rushed up the steps of the imposing town house. It
was a three-storey Georgian building in a grand city
square with a private park in the centre. She rang
the bell and thumped the door knocker as well, so
desperate was she to reach her son.

An older woman with an expressionless face answered the door.

'My son was left here…accidentally,' Pixie said
with a shaky smile. 'I'm here to collect him.'

In silence the door widened, allowing her to step
into a cool, elegant hall. A fleeting glance was all

it took for Pixie to feel shabby, poor and out of her comfort zone as she stood there clad in her cheap raincoat and scuffed trainers. The aromatic scent of beeswax polish lingered in the air, perfectly matching the gracious interior of polished antiques and a truly splendid classical marble sculpture that looked as though it should be in a museum.

'I will ask if Mr Sarantos is free to see you,' the woman said loftily.

As Pixie hovered, she saw two men in suits standing almost out of sight down a short side corridor, both men avidly studying her, and she flushed and turned her head away, relieved when the older woman reappeared and asked her to follow her.

A clammy feeling of disquiet engulfed Pixie's body, quickening both her heartbeat and her breathing as she contemplated the unpleasant prospect of meeting Tor Sarantos again. A man who had utterly rejected her during her pregnancy, who insisted he didn't recall ever even meeting her before? Of course, she didn't want to see him again.

But, sadly for her, Jordan had made it impossible for her to continue sitting on the fence and avoiding the issue of Alfie's existence and his father's responsibility towards him. Now she had to come clean about events eighteen months earlier, regardless of how embarrassing or humiliating that might be. Pixie lifted her chin and reminded herself that all she should still feel guilty about was surrendering to a meaningless sexual encounter while neglecting to protect herself from the risk of a pregnancy.

That horrid little scene in Tor's office had clawed away the finer feelings of guilt that he had once induced in her. Going through a pregnancy and the delivery of her child with only Eloise's occasional support as a friend had made Pixie less self-critical. She had done all right alone; she might not have done brilliantly but there were many who would have coped worse and complained a great deal more. She had nothing to apologise for, she told herself bracingly.

Tor was in a very grim mood. He didn't like mysteries or unexpected developments and the instant the same woman who had forced her way into his office the previous year appeared in his office doorway, a chill of foreboding slid down his rigid spine. Who the hell was she? Stymied by the lack of information about her that day, he had failed to establish her identity after the event and had waited impatiently to see if any claim for child support arrived with his lawyers. When no such claim had arrived, he had written off her visit to a possible mental-health issue. But if she was the child's mother, who was the man surveillance had on tape who had left the child on the doorstep?

'I'm here to pick up my son,' Pixie announced stiffly, her slim shoulders rigid because being even the depth of a room away from Tor Sarantos was too close for comfort. 'I'm sorry you've been dragged into this…er…situation.'

There he stood, tall, poised, predatory dark eyes locked to her like grappling hooks seeking purchase in her tender skin. He was angry, suspicious, everything she didn't want to be forced to deal with but, even with him in that mood, she wasn't impervious to how gorgeous he was, clad in an impossibly elegant dark grey designer suit, sharply tailored to his lean, powerful frame. And while still being that aware of his movie-star-hot looks annoyed her, it also reminded her of how very strange it was that she could ever have conceived a child with a man so far out of her league.

That night they had been together so briefly loomed like a distant and surreal fantasy in the back of her mind and her face heated with mortification because *that* night was the very last thing she wanted to think about in his presence.

'You need to come in, take a seat and explain what you describe as a "situation" to me,' Tor said coolly, watching her like a hawk.

She was incredibly tiny and curvy with a torrent of golden curls that framed her heart-shaped face and enhanced her crystal-blue eyes. Something about her eyes struck him as weirdly familiar; there was something too about that soft, full, pink mouth and the stirring of that vague chord of familiarity spooked Tor as much as a gun held to his head. Because Pixie Miller, whoever she was, was *not* his type. He had always gone for tall brunettes and certainly not a tiny blonde, who from a distance could probably still be mistaken for a child.

'I don't want to talk to you... I just want to collect my son,' Pixie told him truthfully.

'I'm afraid it's not that simple. I need to know what's going on here and then I need to contact social services.'

'Why would you need to contact them?' Pixie gasped in dismay, the colour draining from her face.

'Come in, sit down,' Tor repeated steadily, wondering why she was so skittish and reluctant to speak up when presumably the baby had been dropped as a most effective way of grabbing his attention and forcing such a meeting. 'And then we can talk.'

Pixie clenched her teeth together hard and steeled herself to walk into the book-lined room. He planted a seat down in front of his desk and tapped it.

Pixie slung him a mutinous glance. 'I'm not sitting down while you stand over me,' she warned him. 'Where's my son?'

'In a safe environment being cared for by a nanny. If it makes you feel more secure, I will sit down as well,' Tor breathed impatiently, stepping back behind his desk and dropping down into the leather office chair there.

'You mentioned social services,' Pixie reminded him tautly. *'Why?'*

Tor ignored the question. First, he wanted some facts. 'Who was the man who left the baby outside this house?'

Pixie stiffened. 'My half-brother, Jordan. We had an argument…er…a misunderstanding,' she corrected uncomfortably.

'Why here? Why this house?' Tor pressed.

'Jordan knows you're Alfie's father,' Pixie murmured flatly, focusing on a gold pen lying on the desktop.

'And how could he possibly know that when *I* don't know it?' Tor enquired very drily. 'Am I the victim of some silly story you have told your brother about how you got pregnant?'

Pixie compressed her lips and paled. 'No. I tried to tell you last year at your office, but I bottled out when you didn't even remember me,' she admitted plainly, feeling the shame and sting of that moment warming her cheeks afresh. 'That was a bit too much of a challenge for me.'

His sleek ebony brows had drawn together as he studied her, dark eyes flaming like melted caramel below his outrageous lashes, those beautiful eyes that she had been seduced by that unforgettable night. 'Let's get this straight.' In shock at her simple explanation, Tor regressed a step. 'You are saying that that baby is *mine*?'

'Yes,' Pixie said simply.

'I am finding that hard to credit when I don't remember you. Yes, there is a certain familiarity about your eyes, possibly your face, but that's *all*.'

'So sorry I wasn't a more memorable event,' Pixie countered thinly. 'But facts are facts. You were with me and you got me pregnant.'

'I never have sex without contraception.'

Pixie flung her head back, anger in her gaze. 'Well, you did with me and Alfie is the result. Maybe it was wrong of me not to see a solicitor while I was still pregnant and make some sort of formal approach to you but it's bad enough having to tell you about it, never mind some total stranger! But there it is, that night happened even though we both regret it.'

Tor sprang upright, outraged by the words spilling from her lips. He didn't sleep around indiscriminately, and he was always careful and responsible when sex was involved. 'I still find this story almost impossible to credit and think it may be wiser for us to proceed through legal channels…'

'Oh, for goodness' sake,' Pixie groaned, tipping her head forward and then pushing her hands through her tumbled curls to push the strands off her face again. 'I'm not being fair to you, am I? If you honestly don't remember, it's *because* you were drunk and grieving…although, in my defence, I have to say that I didn't realise how drunk you were until afterwards.'

Tor had frozen in place, a darkening expression of consternation tightening his lean, dark features. 'Drunk? *Grieving?* I rarely drink to excess.'

'It was the anniversary of your wife and child's accident,' Pixie filled in heavily. 'You told me that you went out every year on that date and drank while you remembered them.'

With difficulty, Tor forced himself back down stiffly into his chair. Inside he was reeling with shock, but that she knew that much about him literally confirmed his worst fears and struck him like a hammer blow. How much had he told her? *All* of it or only some of it? He was affronted by his own failure to keep his secrets where they belonged.

'And it's probably very rude to say it…but when you're drunk, you're a much nicer, more approachable guy,' Pixie whispered apologetically. 'If you'd been like you are now, I probably wouldn't have made love with you, which of course would have been wiser for all of us…although I couldn't ever give up Alfie, even to make you feel better.'

'Make *me* feel better?' Tor echoed in disbelief. 'Nothing you have so far told me could make me feel better!'

'Yes, you're one of those glass half-empty rather than half-full types, aren't you?' Pixie sighed.

'Look, now we've got the embarrassing stuff out of the way, can I please see my son?'

'I'm afraid it isn't that straightforward.'

'Why not?' Pixie demanded. 'What's the problem?'

'Where were *you* when your brother took your son and left him in the street?'

'I was in bed.' Pixie flushed beneath his censorious gaze. 'I'm a nurse and I'd just come off night shift. I come home, feed and dress Alfie and then I leave him in Jordan's care while I sleep. I'm usually up by lunchtime. I can get by on very little sleep. And Jordan didn't leave Alfie in the street.'

'He *did*,' Tor interposed flatly.

'Yes, but he hung around somewhere nearby to ensure that Alfie was taken into the house before he left. Look, I *know* that what Jordan did was totally wrong and dangerous and that he shouldn't have done it. I'm still very angry about it too,' Pixie declared tautly. 'But the point is, Jordan has been helping me to look after Alfie and letting us live with him ever since Alfie was born. I owe my brother a lot.'

'I can understand that.'

'No, not really, how could you? You can't understand when you live like *this*...' Pixie shifted an expressive, almost scornful hand that encompassed all the opulent designer touches that distinguished the decor even in a home office setting. 'You and me? We live in very different worlds. In my world it's a struggle to keep a roof over our heads and pay the bills.'

'We will deal with all those problems at a more appropriate time,' Tor cut in. 'Right now I am more concerned about the child's present welfare and security.'

'Alfie's none of your business,' Pixie told him curtly, compressing her lips so hard they went white. 'Do you think I don't appreciate how you feel about this situation? Do you really think I want anything from a man who would prefer that neither I nor my child even exists? '

'This is all getting very emotional and again it is not the right time for this discussion,' Tor countered grimly. 'If your child is also *my* child, I obviously don't want to involve the social services in this issue. But neither am I prepared to hand over custody of a baby to someone who may not keep him safe from harm.'

'How dare you?' Pixie gasped, leaping up out of her seat in angry disbelief at that condemnation.

'Whether you like it or not, you have given me the right to interfere. Either I'm acting as a concerned citizen or as a possible father to ensure that the baby is protected. You can see your son but I will *not* allow you to remove him from this household or take him anywhere near your brother until I am convinced that that is in *his* best interests,' Tor completed with harsh conviction.

'You can't do that…' Pixie whispered shakily.

'Either you accept my conditions, or I contact the authorities, explain what has happened and allow them to make the decisions. If you choose the second option, be aware that neither of us can control events in that scenario,' Tor warned her.

'You don't even believe that Alfie is yours yet,' she protested tightly. 'Why are you trying to screw up our lives? Alfie's a happy child.'

'I want your permission to carry out DNA testing,' Tor admitted. 'I want irrefutable proof of whether or not he is my child.'

'Of course, you're not going to take my word for it,' Pixie remarked stiffly.

Tor was tempted to say that once, without even asking the question, he had blithely assumed that a child was his and had then learnt, very much to his shock, that it was not an assumption any man could afford to make. Now he took nothing for granted and he checked and double-checked everything and trusting anyone had become a serious challenge.

'Will you agree to the testing?' he prompted.

Pixie nodded jerkily for she could think of no good reason to avoid the process. He had the right to know to his own satisfaction that Alfie was his son and it would be wrong of her to deny him that validation, wouldn't it be? Unhappily, however, events were moving far too fast in a direction she had not foreseen.

She had been foolishly naïve when she'd raced to Tor's home to collect her son, too distraught to appreciate that there would be long-term consequences to such exposure. Tor would not let either of them walk away again until his questions were answered. And evidently, she had misjudged him that day at his office. He *had* forgotten her as entirely as though she had never existed and that was an unwelcome truth that could only hurt.

As she watched, he pulled out a phone, selected a number and began speaking to someone in a foreign language. She wondered if it was Greek while she scanned the eloquent movement of a lean brown hand, fingers spreading and then curling as he talked. For such a tall, well-built guy he was very graceful, but all his movements were tense and controlled, hinting at the darkness of his mood.

The night they had met Tor had been so natural, so relaxed and open with her. Sober, however, he was a very different person with his freezing politeness and disciplined reserve. But she could still read him well enough to recognise that her appearance and that of a potential child in his life were a huge surprise and a disaster on his terms. He didn't *want* Alfie. He might be talking impressively about needing to ensure that Alfie was safe, but he wasn't personally interested in her son, excited at the possibility of being his father, or indeed anything positive that she could see.

'I've organised the DNA testing,' he informed her grimly. 'Now I want you to sit back down and tell me about the night we met.'

'No...' Pixie's refusal leapt straight to her lips.

'But obviously I want to know what happened between us!' Tor slung back at her between gritted teeth.

'Why should you need to know anything when Alfie's the evidence?' Pixie dared, lifting her chin.

'So, you expect me to just live with this blank space in my memory?' Tor breathed with incredulous bite.

'Yes, I'm quite happy to exist in that blank and I don't see any advantage to raking over an encounter that upsets you so much.'

'I'm *not* upset,' Tor responded icily.

'Angry, ashamed, whatever you want to call it. It doesn't matter to me now,' Pixie told him truthfully, wishing he could bring himself to be a little more honest with her. 'All I want now is to see my son.'

Tor released his breath in a soundless hiss of frustration. He wasn't accustomed to dealing with opposition from a woman. Women invariably went out of their way to please and flatter him, keen to attract and retain his interest. But Pixie Miller?

She was more likely to raise her stubborn chin and challenge him with defiant crystal-blue eyes. And he wondered, *of course*, he wondered if it had been that difference in her that had attracted him to her in the first place. Was he attracted to stronger, more independent women? Certainly, he never had been in the past, had always played safe by choosing quiet, discreet lovers who understood that sex with him didn't ever lead to anything deeper.

But that he should have slept with another woman that night of all nights? That shook him, but it also filled him with intense curiosity. He might not know her, but he knew himself. Either Pixie had been extraordinarily seductive, or she was something a great deal more special than she was willing to admit or he was able to remember...

CHAPTER FOUR

'I THINK YOU could at least take your coat off before I take you upstairs to your son.' Tor told Pixie drily. 'You won't be returning home until we sort this out.'

With a stiff little twist of her shoulders, Pixie removed her coat. 'There's nothing to sort and I have to be back at work by seven.'

'Leaving the baby in your brother's tender care? Not on my watch,' Tor spelt out curtly, watching her bend to drape the coat over the chair and reveal an awesomely curvy bottom covered in tight denim. Grabbable, squeezable, touchable, every word that occurred to him startled him because he was no longer a sexually libidinous teenager and he didn't leer at women's bodies like one either, did he? Well, so much for Pixie Miller not being his type, a little devil piped up in the back of his brain, infuriating him even more as a throbbing pulse at his groin stirred.

She was sexy, *very* sexy, that was all it was, and

her appeal was all the stronger because she didn't work at it. No, there was nothing remotely inviting or sensual about her presentation of herself, he conceded grudgingly, nothing in her appearance that sought attention. She looked like what she was: a young mother on a restricted income. But that description did not encompass the whole of her or reveal the charm of those tousled golden curls, the clarity of her bright anxious eyes, the soft pink pout of her mouth.

Angrily aware of his burgeoning erection, Tor led the way out of the room and up the sweeping staircase. He hadn't even looked at the child, hadn't gone near it. If he was honest with himself for once, that was because he tended to avoid young children and the memories they roused of Sofia.

Now in many ways, though, he was being confronted by his worst nightmare: another child and a relationship with a woman that could not be denied, the sort of bonds he had been resolutely determined to avoid since the death of his wife and daughter.

Of course, her son could not be his! At the very least it was highly unlikely. Had he even *had* sex with her that night? There was still room for doubt on that score. He had few memories of that anniversary, had already acknowledged that he had behaved irresponsibly by getting dangerously drunk. He had wakened with an aching head in an unfamiliar bedroom, but he had *still* been fully clothed.

That he could have had sex with anyone had not once occurred to him, only that he shouldn't have been reckless enough to get that intoxicated. As he had left that strange house in haste, someone had been coming downstairs behind him and he hadn't even turned his head because all he had wanted to do was get home. He had known even at that point that he would not be drowning himself in alcohol for that anniversary ever again. It had been a foolish, juvenile habit he had naturally decided not to repeat.

'They're in here…' Tor thrust open the door.

Pixie surged over the threshold. Standing up, Alfie was holding on to the side of a travel cot and bouncing with his usual irrepressible energy. He was the strangest mix of his parental genes, she thought fondly, because he had inherited her golden curls with his father's dark eyes and olive skin tone.

'Mm…mm…mm!' Alfie burbled excitedly, his sturdy little arms lifting as soon as he saw his mother.

'I think he's trying to say Mum,' the smiling young woman hovering said. 'Hello, I'm Emma and I've been looking after your…son?'

Alfie clawed up the front of Pixie's body in his desperation to reach her and held on as tight as a clam with his whole body wrapped round her, burying his little face fearfully in her shoulder, still muttering, 'Mm. .mm.'

It was the moment when Pixie would have happily killed her brother for having subjected her child to such a frightening experience. Alfie wasn't normally clingy, and she had never seen him frightened before because he was one of those unnerving kids who jumped unafraid into unfamiliar situations and left her with her heart in her mouth.

'Alfie,' Pixie sighed, hugging him close. 'Hello, Emma. I'm Pixie and, yes, I'm his mum and this little boy got lost this morning and I was frantic!' She punctuated those remarks by tickling Alfie under the ribs in an effort to break him free of his anxiety and it worked. Alfie went off into paroxysms of giggles and leant back, the weight of him forcing Pixie to kneel down and brace him on the floor before he toppled both of them.

'He's a real little charmer,' Emma commented. 'How old is he?'

'Nine months.'

'And already getting ready to walk. My goodness, that'll be a challenge for you,' Emma chattered. 'The younger they are, the less sense they have.'

Tor had frozen where he stood as Alfie flung his head back, laughing, and his dancing dark eyes and slanting mischievous grin reminded Tor powerfully of his youngest brother, Kristo, who was only seventeen. Unnerved by that instantaneous sense of familial recognition, he looked hastily away, re-

minding himself that the child was very unlikely
to be related to him. But if he *was*?

A faint shudder raked through Tor's tall, powerful frame because *that* would be a game-changer,
the ultimate game-changer, forcing him to embrace
everything he had turned his back on. Choice would
have nothing to do with it.

'This is Alfie,' Pixie said simply as she looked
up at Tor, so impossibly tall from that angle as she
knelt. He looked pale, or as pale as someone as sun
bronzed as he was could look, she adjusted uncomfortably.

Alfie settled back on the floor to explore a plastic
truck with his fingers and his mouth, his attention
unnervingly locked to Tor as if he was sizing him
up. Tor wanted to back away. Countless memories
of Sofia at the same age were engulfing him but he
fought them off and got down on his knees, careless of his suit and his dignity.

'Shall I leave now, Mr Sarantos?' the nanny enquired.

'No, we still need you, but you can take a break
while Alfie has his mother here,' Tor murmured,
quite proud of the steadiness of his voice as Emma
nodded and left the room.

Alfie settled the truck down on Tor's thigh and
sat back expectantly, big chocolate-coloured eyes
unerringly pinned to Tor, almost as though he could
sense his discomfiture.

'Let me,' Pixie began to intervene awkwardly.

'No, I've got this.' Alfie chuckled as Tor ran the truck along the floor with the appropriate *vroom-vroom* noises even though his eyes stung like mad as he did it and he cursed himself for being a sentimental fool.

Alfie grinned and patted Tor's thigh to indicate that he wanted his truck back now that its magic had been demonstrated to his satisfaction. Tor handed it back and hastily backed away, vaulting back upright again.

'I'm sorry… I'm out of practice. I've avoided young children since, well, since Sofia's death,' he admitted grittily, determined to be frank because he had evidently been more than frank with this young woman when they first met and for once there was no reason for him to put up a front.

Pixie almost winced because that likelihood hadn't occurred to her, and she scolded herself for not appreciating that Alfie would resurrect memories that Tor probably preferred to bury. Even so, on another level and one she didn't want to examine, his sensitivity saddened her because Alfie was his child too. Of course, he wouldn't accept that until he had the official proof of it.

With a knock on the door the woman who appeared to be the housekeeper appeared and announced that Tor had a visitor downstairs.

'I'll send him up when he's done with me. It'll be the DNA testing I requested.'

'My goodness, how did you get it organised this quickly?' Pixie exclaimed in surprise.

'To put it simply…money talks,' Tor replied drily. 'But I'm afraid we'll still have to wait twenty-four hours for the results.'

'Well, I'm not going to be in suspense,' Pixie pointed out.

'You haven't the slightest doubt?'

Pixie reddened and then lifted her head high, her crystal-blue eyes awash with censure.

'No. You were my first and only, so there isn't the smallest chance that anyone else could have fathered Alfie.'

His lean, darkly handsome features tightened as though she had struck him, and she might as well have done, Tor acknowledged. He paused at the door and glanced back at her. 'How old are you?'

'Twenty-two,' Pixie answered. 'You asked me the same question the night we met. It's infuriating. It's because I'm small and people always assume I'm younger than I am.'

Tor went downstairs to have the swab done for the DNA testing with an inescapable sense of guilt. If that little boy was his child, he had hit on a twenty-one-year-old virgin, left her to struggle through her pregnancy alone, denied all knowledge of her when she'd approached him for support and generally treated her in the most unforgivable manner. The idea that he could have behaved like that shattered him and left him reeling with shock because the whole nightmare situation was making him appreciate that he hadn't been living in the *real* world for over six years.

He had been living in the past, seeing the world and the people around him through toxic lenses, believing that he was standing tall and strong in the face of adversity when in fact he was continually backing away from the wounding truth that his wife and his half-brother had betrayed him. He hadn't come to terms with it, hadn't dealt with it, hadn't put it behind him the way he should have done.

And in reacting in that inflexible way, it seemed he might have caused one hell of a lot of damage to an innocent bystander. He breathed in deep and slow as he made those deductions and hoped that the child turned out not to be his, because at that moment the alternative was just too much for him to contemplate.

The DNA test was carried out in minutes and Pixie was left alone with her son. After some energetic play, Alfie went down in the travel cot for a nap. She had put her phone on mute because Jordan had called her repeatedly and she wasn't in the mood to talk to him and didn't know what she would say when she did. He had destroyed her trust in him but to a certain extent she understood his frustration with her.

She had leant on her brother when she should've been seeking the support of Alfie's father because her pride had got in the way and that stubborn pride of hers hadn't done her any favours.

For months, Jordan had been forced to stay home most evenings while she was at work, a considerable sacrifice for a young, single man. Worse still, he was unable to look for other employment because only casual barista work allowed him to choose his hours and mind Alfie for his sister. Her decision to go ahead and have her child had adversely affected Jordan's life. It was pointless to say that she had never meant to do that when she had still gone ahead and done what *she* wanted to do, which was to give birth to a child without a partner and depend on her brother's help.

If she could have gone back and changed things she knew she would have done it all differently, she conceded heavily. She had taxed her brother's patience for too long, forcing him to act in an effort to make her confront Tor. Yes, dumping Alfie on Tor's doorstep had been absolutely the wrong way to go about achieving that, but had she gone to a solicitor to claim child support from Tor, Jordan might have been released from the responsibility of having to help her look after her child months ago.

'Mr Sarantos would like you to come downstairs

for a meal,' Emma told her, sliding into the room on quiet feet. 'I'll keep an eye on Alfie.'

Pixie checked the time and suppressed a sigh. Soon she would need to get home to get ready for work. As she came down into the hall the housekeeper was waiting to show her into a formal dining room, where a polished table set with silver cutlery and crystal wine glasses awaited her. Tor strolled forward, all lithe contained power, vibrant energy radiating from his dark golden eyes.

'I assumed you'd be hungry.'

'I've haven't got much time before we have to leave,' Pixie responded uncomfortably.

'I still want to know what happened that night between us,' Tor admitted, disconcerting her.

'But it's not important now,' Pixie reasoned stiffly.

'If you're telling me the truth and that night led to the conception of my son, it's *very* important,' Tor contradicted as a man in a short white jacket entered and proceeded to pour the wine, mercifully silencing him on that subject.

'Not for me, thank you,' Pixie said, refusing the wine while watching the man leave again with wide eyes. 'You are surrounded by staff here.'

'I have to concentrate on work. Domestic staff take the irritating small stuff out of my day. How do you feel about leaving Alfie here in Emma's care tonight?'

Pixie paled. 'I'd prefer to take him home.'

'Which would mean your brother taking charge of him again. Give your brother a night off,' Tor urged.

Her slight shoulders stiffened. She had to talk to Jordan before she could feel that she could trust him again with her child. 'If I didn't have to go to work, I wouldn't agree,' she muttered ruefully. 'But just one night, and I'll have to go home and get Alfie's things before.'

'Anything the baby needs can be bought.'

'Bunny, his toy rabbit, can't be, and he won't go down for the night without it. Babies like familiar things around them. It makes them feel secure.' Pixie sighed. 'I also need to feed my cat and if Alfie stays, when am I supposed to get him back tomorrow?'

'I'm expecting you to return here in the morning and stay. A room beside his will be prepared for your use. It would also mean that you'll be here when the DNA results become available.'

He already had her movements and Alfie's all worked out on his schedule, but letting him interfere in their lives to that extent disturbed Pixie. On the other hand, Tor contacting the authorities to share his concern about Alfie's safety in her brother's custody would cause a firestorm, which would be a great deal worse, she conceded wryly. In truth, with that 'concerned citizen' threat of his, Tor Sarantos had trapped her between a rock and a hard place and deprived her of choice.

'That night…' Tor said again, shimmering dark golden eyes locking to her and making it hard for her to find her voice.

And Pixie gave way but stuck to the bare bones, telling him about their meeting in the kitchen, the cheese toasted sandwich she had given him and the accidental collision he had had with the cupboard door. While she talked, a deliciously cooked meal was served, and she began to eat.

'Yes… I had a bruise above my eye,' Tor commented with a frown. 'I wondered if I'd fallen or got into some sort of altercation.'

'The taxi didn't arrive and that was my fault too,' Pixie explained in a rush. 'I was only staying there for two weeks and when you asked me for the house number I got it wrong. I only realised that a couple of days afterwards.'

'These are dry facts,' Tor remarked, cradling his wine glass elegantly in one lean brown hand as he lounged back in his chair like a king surveying a recalcitrant subject. 'You've stripped everything personal out of this account. Nothing you have yet shared explains how we ended up in bed together.'

'I should think your imagination could fill in that particular blank,' Pixie dared.

'Surprisingly not. That particular night I wouldn't

have been looking for sex with anyone,' Tor asserted coolly. 'It was out of character.'

'Blame the alcohol.'

'And as you were a virgin, presumably it was out of character for you as well.'

Pixie went red as fire and hated him for throwing that in her teeth. 'Obviously, I was overwhelmingly attracted to you.'

An entirely spontaneous grin slashed Tor's wide sensual mouth, chasing the gravity from his startlingly handsome features. 'OK.'

'Was that *personal* enough for you?' Pixie slammed back at him sharply as she rose from the table, furious that he had embarrassed her and that she had been that honest with him in her response.

As Tor also sprang up, smouldering dark golden eyes collided with hers and she stopped breathing and froze in her retreat to the door. She couldn't drag her attention from him as he stalked towards her, all lean predatory grace and masculine power.

'No, in the interests of research I'd like to get a lot more personal,' Tor confided. 'I want to kiss you.'

Pixie was knocked off balance entirely by that familiar phrase. 'You said that that night.'

'And what did you say?'

'*Do it,*' she recalled weakly as he reached for her.

The tip of his tongue licked along the closed seam of her mouth and she shivered violently, wanting more, craving more, outraged by the flood of instant awareness cascading through her treacherous body. She didn't know what he did to her self-discipline, but it was lethal because with one touch her whole body switched on as though he had pressed a magic button. Her skin felt too tight round her bones, her breath shortened in her throat and her heart began to pound. The light play of his splayed fingers across her spine somehow made her breasts swell and stir inside her bra, letting her feel the straining tautness of her nipples. Her lips parted and he took advantage, delving between to explore the moist interior of her mouth.

The immediate rush of heat and dampness between her thighs took her by storm, prickling, tingling awareness shooting through every nerve ending she possessed. She jerked in helpless response. It was one kiss and her body leapt on it as though it were her first meal after a famine.

He pressed her back against the table and her hands lifted up, her fingers spearing into his springy black hair to hold him fast while his firm lips moved with compelling hunger on hers. The bottom could've fallen out of the world at that moment and she wouldn't have noticed. Her surroundings had fallen away. All she was aware of was him, the hard, demanding bar of his erection against her stomach, the passion of his mouth on hers, the glorious heat and strength of him that close.

Breathing raggedly, Tor dragged his mouth from her and pulled back from her, dark eyes flaring with bright golden intensity and full of new knowledge. 'Well. I don't need to ask *how* it happened, do I? We have explosive chemistry…and I'm remembering things now. The taste of you…and green hair? *Diavole*…where does *green* hair come into it? And I said that you reminded me of a forest fairy? *Thee mou*…spouting nonsense of that calibre, I must've been incredibly drunk'

Pixie reeled back from him, deeply shaken by the passion that had betrayed her in his arms, exposing a vulnerability that mortified her. She didn't even feel relieved that he was starting to remember stuff, only more mortified and exposed than ever.

'I had dyed my hair before we met…it stayed sort of pale green until it finally washed out,' she muttered tightly. 'And you *did* compare me to a forest fairy, but only because someone else said I reminded them of a leprechaun with my green hair and I told you that.'

Tor shot her a glance of concealed wonderment because she was on another plane entirely, too naïve to even register how unusual it was to find a sexual connection that strong. He had gone up in flames with her. She was a dynamite charge in a tiny package and all he had wanted to do was spread her out on the table and thrust inside her hard and fast.

The ache of having to deny and control his libido

was new to him. Sex had become something Tor snapped his fingers and received with minimal effort. Persuading or coaxing had never been required from him. But no woman had ever aroused him to the extent that Pixie did. Her effect on him, however, certainly explained what must have happened that night and his own unusual recklessness...

But he had recalled enough of his own reactions to be thoroughly disconcerted by what he was both learning and remembering. *Best sex I ever had...* That was what he had fallen asleep thinking that night, satiated by the glory of her silken, tight depths. He breathed in deep and slow, tamping down those thoughts and forcing himself back to the present.

'A limo will take you home and bring you back here again. Do you want me to accompany you? At some stage, I will need to speak to your brother,' Tor imparted, while thinking that within a couple of days he would know everything he needed to know about the siblings because he had told his head of security to have them checked out.

'Why would you need to speak to Jordan?'

Tor compressed his lips. 'Because you don't appear to have sufficient control over him.'

Her face flamed with annoyance because she was in no position to argue after what Jordan had done with Alfie.

'Look, with Emma here I'll let Alfie stay here

tonight and I'll come back in the morning as you asked but, to be frank, once the emergency is over, I hope we can all settle back down and get on with our lives,' Pixie admitted, hoping that if she gave a little, he would too. 'But I don't want you to speak to Jordan. I'll take care of that.'

'How?' Tor challenged.

'I can't defend what Jordan did this morning when he left Alfie here,' Pixie conceded. 'But he's my half-brother, my only surviving family and he's been good to both of us when there was nobody else willing to help, so please cut him some slack...'

'If that baby *is* my son, it's going to change your lives,' Tor retorted in a growling undertone, ignoring her plea on her brother's behalf. 'I'd be a liar if I said anything else.'

Pixie set her teeth firmly together on a hasty and ill-judged response to that statement. She saw no reason why he should interfere with *her* life. She was willing to accept him as a masculine role model in Alfie's world and hopefully a better one than Jordan had so far proved to be. Presumably, Tor would expect to spend time with Alfie. He would also expect to contribute towards his support, she assumed, but she hoped that that would be as far as his interference went because there was nothing more personal between them than that single night and Alfie's unintentional conception.

Really? a little voice sniped, unimpressed, deep

inside her. What about that kiss? What about that
response you gave him? That had gone way beyond
masculine role models and child support, that had
been personal and intimate to a level that filled Pixie
with guilt and discomfiture. That kiss had smashed
through the defensive barriers she had forged and
blown her away.

'Why did you call him Alfie?'

'I named him after my grandfather. He was a
wonderful character. He died when I was six, but I
never forgot him.'

Tor accompanied her to the front door, waiting
there in silence until a sleek black shiny limousine
pulled up outside. 'I have an appointment now, so
I won't see you before you leave for work. Hopefully, I'll see you in the morning for breakfast,' he
murmured silkily.

Pixie nodded and went down the steps, wide-
eyed as the driver climbed out to open the passenger
door of the limousine for her. She got in, sinking
into the pearl-grey leather upholstery and scanning
the embellishments in front of her, wondering what
the various buttons and switches she could see did,
but restraining herself from experimenting lest she
embarrass herself.

The house was empty when she got back. Jordan had gone out, probably to avoid dealing with
her recriminations, she reflected with a wry shake
of her head. She rushed around, gathering up her

son's belongings, and changed for work, conscious that she didn't have much time to waste.

If that baby is my son, it's going to change your lives.

That declaration had aggravated her. Tor Sarantos could only change what she *allowed* him to change, she reminded herself bracingly. He didn't own her, he didn't own either of them. He couldn't force her to do *anything* she didn't want to do…

CHAPTER FIVE

ELOISE SAT ACROSS the table in the hospital canteen from Pixie during their break and said, 'About the only thing your brother got right was when he advised you to take what you can get to make raising Alfie easier. His father *should* be sharing the responsibility.'

Pixie stiffened and blinked, taken aback by the pretty brunette's frankly offered opinion. Since the other nurse and her brother had broken up, by mutual agreement both women had avoided discussing Jordan. 'I never thought you'd say that.'

'It's gloves-off time. The best thing for both you and Alfie would be to get as far away from Jordan as you can because if you don't, he'll rob you blind like he did me.' Eloise sighed. 'I'm sorry to be that blunt, Pixie, but Jordan left me broke. Although I could never get the truth out of him, money was always disappearing, and I didn't believe the stories he told me. I suspected he was gambling but he laughed in my face when I accused him, and I couldn't prove anything. If Alfie's father gives you financial help, grab it with both hands and step away from your brother.'

'*Gambling?*' Pixie whispered, aghast.

'What else could he be at? Where do you think the debts he's always complaining about are coming from?' Eloise prompted in an undertone, mindful of the diners at tables nearby. 'He doesn't live the high life or smoke or use drugs. The money has to be going somewhere and, if you're not careful, you and Alfie will end up on the street because when I moved out that mortgage was already in serious arrears.'

Pixie frowned. 'But I give him most of the money to cover it every month.'

'Check it out for yourself. Your name's on the mortgage too,' Eloise reminded her drily. 'Stop trusting Jordan to take care of the budget because I suspect he's been pulling the wool over your eyes as well.'

'You think he's dishonest. That's why you dumped him,' Pixie finally grasped and that new knowledge made her feel grossly uncomfortable. 'But if he *was* that kind of cheating, lying person, why would he have looked after me for so long?'

The brunette rolled her eyes ruefully. 'Everyone's a mix of good and bad. But you had better believe that your brother dumped your son on his rich father's doorstep because he decided that there was something in it for *him*!'

'I wish you'd told me what you suspected sooner,' Pixie admitted heavily, having been given a lot to think about. It was an empty wish, but she found herself wishing that her parents were still alive because she would have turned to them for advice. She felt gutted by the suspicion that Jordan might have been up to no good behind her back and that he could not be trusted with money.

'Jordan and I split up and bad-mouthing him to his sister afterwards struck me as bitchy and unnecessary because I've moved on now.'

After that conversation, it was a struggle for Pixie to concentrate on work and when she was leaving the hospital, with her brain buzzing with conjecture, she was dismayed to see Jordan waiting for her outside the door because she still wasn't ready to deal with him. At the same time, though, she knew it was necessary.

Her brother gave her a sad-eyed sideways glance. 'I'm sorry,' he said awkwardly as he walked by her side. 'But I didn't have a choice—'

'There's *always* a choice, Jordan!' Pixie cut in thinly.

'No, on this occasion there truly wasn't,' Jordan told her, dropping down onto a stone bench that overlooked the busy car park. 'You ignored all my advice. You refused to go to a solicitor and apply for child support.'

'I know *but*—' Pixie deemed it too early in the conversation to admit that she now accepted she had leant too heavily on him for support.

'The house is about to be repossessed,' Jordan told her heavily.

Pixie turned bone white. 'That's not possible. There would have been letters.'

'I've been hiding the letters. I hoped that I could stop it happening, but I can't, and I *had* to force you to deal with Sarantos some way, so that he could be there to look after you and Alfie. I didn't want you ending up in some homeless shelter because I've been stupid!'

Pixie's knees finally gave way and she sat down beside him, plunged deep into shock by that blunt confession. 'But I've been giving you money towards the payment every month.'

'It's all gone. I'm sorry but we're going to lose the house,' Jordan muttered heavily.

As he confirmed Eloise's misgivings, Pixie was reeling in horror and disbelief at such a betrayal of her trust. 'But how could that happen?'

Her brother sprang up again, refusing to meet her stricken gaze. 'I'm very sorry,' he said again and he walked away at speed.

Pixie splurged on another taxi to return to Tor's town house. She was in a state and her exhaustion wasn't helping. Worry about her brother's state of mind and the fear of impending homelessness had overloaded her brain. Only a couple of days ago she had been secure and now all of a sudden, and without warning, her life was falling apart. Once again she craved parental support. Jordan had lied to her and could no longer be trusted. In the aftermath of that acknowledgement, walking into the gracious luxury of Tor's home gave her a surreal feeling and, more than ever, the sense that she did not belong in such a setting.

She went straight upstairs and found Emma bathing Alfie. That reunion got her very damp, but she insisted on taking over because early mornings had always been her fun time with Alfie, and she treasured those moments when he was fresh for the new day and full of energy and nonsense.

She took him downstairs for breakfast, wincing at the formality of the dining room and the prospect of Alfie's mealtime messiness, but Mrs James, the housekeeper, did at least have a smile for her as a high chair was brought in—complete, she was amused to see, with a protective mat for it to sit on.

Tor, it seemed, was already long gone from the house, which was a relief for Pixie in the mood she was in.

After she and Alfie had both eaten their fill from an array of breakfast dishes that would not have shamed a top-flight hotel, she handed her son back to Emma and retired to the beautiful room next door to them, smothering a yawn.

Nothing would seem so bad after she had had a decent sleep, she soothed herself as she climbed into the wonderfully comfortable bed and set the alarm on her phone. Perhaps some solution would come to her while she slept, she thought hopefully, striving not to stress about the future but knowing in her gut that she did not want to be dependent on Tor.

She could share Alfie with him, but she wanted any other connection between them to be remote and unemotional and most definitely *not* physical. The last thing she needed was to get attached to a man still in love with his dead wife, even though she had cheated on him. She hoped she had more sense than that, but a hot, sexy Greek like Tor Sarantos played merry hell with a woman's common sense. She had made a huge mistake once with Tor, but she had no intention of repeating that mistake, she assured herself firmly.

The results of the DNA testing had been delivered to Tor at his office, but he resisted the urge to rip open the envelope. On another level, he knew he didn't really need to open the envelope to know that Alfie was *his* child. That truth had shone out of Pixie when he'd realised that she had no doubts about who had fathered her child, but, even more potently, Tor had felt the family connection the instant he saw Alfie's smile and was reminded of his little brother. The preliminary file he received on Pixie and her brother, however, posed more of a problem. The contents bothered Tor and while he also appreciated that those same facts would make Pixie more reliant on him for assistance, Tor didn't really want to be the bearer of such bad news when his relationship with Alfie's mother was already strained and difficult. On the other hand, he couldn't see that he had much of a choice on that score.

He went home at lunchtime, needing to be within reach of the child he believed to be his, before the results confirmed it. Telling a flustered Mrs James, taken aback by his sudden appearance, that he didn't need lunch, only coffee, he strode into his home office. He tore into the envelope then, and breathed in deep before he looked down at the page in his hand.

Ninety-nine point nine per cent likelihood that he was Alfie's father. Ironically, the shock wave of confirmation left him light-headed and then galvanised him into heading straight upstairs. He glanced down at his immaculate city suit and silk tie and frowned, striding into his bedroom to change.

He was a father, genuinely a father, for the first time. It shook him how much that meant to him. Of course, the first time around he had taken fatherhood for granted. He hadn't realised that until the night Katerina and Sofia died.

Katerina had put the little girl into the car against his wishes while informing him that he had no right to object because Sofia wasn't *his* daughter, but her lover's. Rage had burned in Tor's gut like a bushfire. Never again would he allow a woman to put him in so powerless a position, he'd sworn to himself.

He was a father, and fathers had rights…didn't they? He was an unmarried father, though. That was a different situation. He needed to talk to his legal team to find out exactly where he stood.

But that wasn't an immediate priority, he told himself impatiently, heading straight off to see his son.

Frustratingly, however, Alfie was sound asleep, his little flushed face tucked up against a battered rabbit soft toy, his bottom in the air. Tor studied the slumbering child intently, wanting to pick him up, wanting to hold him, knowing he could not. Phone the lawyers, his ESP was urging as the recollection of his own family history returned to haunt him.

His elder brother, Sevastiano, had grown up outside Tor's family circle because his Italian mother, Francesca, had changed her mind about marrying Tor's father to marry another man instead. Tor's father, Hallas, had moved heaven and earth to try to gain access to the child he had known Francesca was already carrying, but he had failed because a child born within marriage was deemed to be the husband's child and DNA testing had been in its infancy back then. Without evidence that there was a blood tie, the law and an antagonistic stepfather had excluded Hallas from his son's life. That sobering story in mind, Tor phoned his lawyers and, from them, he learned facts that startled him. In the UK, an unmarried father had virtually no rights. He had no right to either custody or even visitation with his child without the mother's consent.

Pixie was emerging from the en suite bathroom wrapped in a capacious towel when a knock sounded on the bedroom door. She had slept like a log but the instant she wakened her mind began seething with anxiety again. If the house was to be repossessed, where was she going to live? How was she going to manage to work without Jordan to rely on for childcare? Checking the towel was secure, she opened the door a crack.

'It's Tor…can we talk?'

'Right now?' Pixie muttered doubtfully, stepping back a few feet without actually meaning him to take that retreat as an invitation.

Tor strode in without skipping a beat. 'Give me five minutes,' he urged.

His gorgeous black-lashed dark eyes locked to her, golden as heated honey, and she froze, scanning his appearance in faded jeans and a black top with almost hungry eagerness. He looked so good in denim he stole her breath from her lungs, the jeans showcasing lean hips and long powerful thighs. She dredged her attention from him again with pink spattering her cheeks and said uneasily, 'I need to get dressed.'

'You're pretty much covered from head to toe,' he pointed out gently.

It was true. The large towel stretched from above her breasts to her feet and she sank down on the side of the bed and endeavoured to relax and behave less awkwardly around him.

'I got the DNA results,' he volunteered. 'And as you said, Alfie's my son.'

'So?' Pixie prompted.

'We have a lot to talk about.'

'I suppose we have…that is *if* you're planning to play an active part in his life,' Pixie responded.

'So far I may not have made much of a showing in the father stakes, but I plan to change that,' Tor swore with impressive resolve.

'I believe that would benefit Alfie,' Pixie commented quietly.

'I hope that it will benefit *both* of you,' Tor countered with assurance, his attention welded to her because she was so tiny and dainty in the towel, her curls damp from the shower, bare pink toes peeping out from beneath it. Impossibly pretty, incredibly cute and sexy. All of a sudden, this tiny blonde was becoming the most fascinating woman he had come across in years. It was *because* she was Alfie's mother, he reasoned with himself, nothing at all to do with the fact that he wanted to rip the towel off her and spread her across the bed. That was just lust, normal, natural lust. It didn't relate to anything more complex.

Colouring at the tenor of his appraisal, Pixie shifted uneasily. 'I'm not sure I understand what you mean…obviously we can learn to be civil to each other,' she murmured. 'It's probably a blessing that we were never in an actual relationship. We've got none of the baggage that can go with that scenario. That's a healthy start.'

Tor didn't agree at all. He didn't want to be reminded that they had never been in a relationship. Nor did he want to be held at arm's length like a stranger.

'I'd like to have my name put on Alfie's birth certificate, but I understand you have to fill in forms and go to court to achieve that.'

'Then you already know more than I do,' Pixie admitted, stiffening a little at that reference to going to court, nervous of that legal step without even knowing why. 'I only know that when I registered his birth I couldn't put your name on the certificate without you being there and agreeing to it.'

'We'll look into it.'

'Look, can I get dressed now?' Pixie pressed. 'I'll come downstairs straight away.'

Tor departed, thinking about the contents of that

file and the brother she semi-idolised for his supposed sacrifice in becoming her guardian. What he had to tell her would hurt, but he could not conceal the truth from her when her safety and his son's could be at risk.

Pixie got dressed, pulling on ankle boots, a flouncy skirt and a long loose sweater. She was off work for a few days and she liked to make the most of her downtime, usually commencing her break with a trip to the park with Alfie and a fancy coffee somewhere. But she didn't have the money to cover fancy coffees any longer, she reminded herself, feeling guilty about the taxis she had employed in recent days. Now she had to carefully conserve what money she had because she had to be prepared to find somewhere else to live. And there and then, the whole towering pack of cards on which her life and security were built began to topple, she acknowledged with a sinking in the pit of her stomach. Her salary was good, but it wouldn't stretch to cover both rent *and* childcare.

Tor awaited her in the opulent drawing room, which had oil paintings on the walls and sumptuous contemporary seating. A tray sat on the tiered coffee table. 'We'll serve ourselves,' he told the housekeeper smoothly.

Tor scanned the outfit Pixie wore, which was eclectic to say the very least, his gaze lingering on her slender, shapely legs and then whipping up to her flushed face beneath the curls she had haphazardly caught up in a knot on top of her head, the hairstyle accentuating her brilliant blue eyes. Natural, artless, everything he had never looked for in a woman, everything he had never guessed he would find appealing.

Pixie dished out the coffee, remembering that he took his black and sweet and handing it to him. She sank down into the depths of a capacious sofa, one knee neatly hooked over the other, her legs slanted to one side while tension thrummed through her, making her small body rigid while she wondered what he wanted to say and what demands he might try to make of her. His name on the birth certificate? She saw no reason to object to that.

'As soon as I realised that you were saying that I was the father of your child yesterday I asked my head of security to have your background investigated—'

'*Investigated?*' Pixie repeated, cutting in, her dismay unhidden.

'I'm sorry if that annoys you, but I needed to know more about you. It's standard in my life to take that sort of precaution,' Tor proffered unapologetically.

Pixie forced an uneasy little smile. 'I've got nothing to hide.'

'No, but unfortunately your brother did,' Tor revealed ruefully.

'If you're about to tell me that the house is about

to be repossessed because of Jordan's debts, I already know. He came to see me after I finished work at the hospital today. It was a major shock because I wasn't aware that there was even a problem. He had hidden that from me.'

'His web of deception goes much deeper than that, I'm afraid,' Tor told her reluctantly.

Fully focused on his tall, powerful figure by the fireplace, Pixie sat forward with a frown. 'What do you mean?'

'When your parents passed away, your mother's house was left entirely to you.'

'No, the house was left to both Jordan and me,' Pixie corrected.

'Obviously, it was in your brother's interests to make you believe that, but that house, which originally belonged to your mother's parents, was left solely to *you*. In fact, so keen was your mother to ensure that the house went to you only that she wrote her will soon after she married Jordan's father, in the event that they should have any children. Social services were aware that the house belonged to you but at the time that Jordan applied to become your guardian he was decently employed and would have seemed to be a fine upstanding citizen, capable of taking care of his little half-sister...'

Her brow furrowed in growing surprise. 'Jordan didn't get a share of the house *too*?'

'No. But by taking on caring for you he gained

access to a free roof over his head and as soon as you were old enough he got you to sign documents which enabled him to take out a large loan against the house.'

Pixie frowned. 'The bathroom and kitchen were badly in need of an update. We both had to sign for the loan.'

'I suspect he gave you forged documents. You were young, inexperienced. I doubt that it took much effort for him to fool you, and at the same time he got you to put him on the mortgage, which enabled him to do a great deal behind your back.'

Pixie blinked rapidly. What he was telling her was much worse than anything she could have dreamt up because he was suggesting that her brother had defrauded her, had taken advantage of her ignorance and *used* her to try to steal *her* inheritance. 'The loan was honest. There was nothing questionable about it,' she argued tightly, seeking a strand of comforting truth to cling to in her turmoil. 'The work needed to be done and there was no other way of paying for it.'

'But Jordan pocketed most of the loan and, I imagine, spent only a small part of it on home improvements. From what I understand that's when the gambling started. He bet, he lost, he borrowed more and more money from various sleazy sources, and he sank deeper and deeper into debt. He's a gambling addict.'

'Then he needs professional help,' she whispered painfully, appalled that Jordan could have sunk so low without her even noticing and wondering what could possibly be done to cure him of such an addiction. She was gutted and she felt horribly alone, for he was her only relative. Yet in her heart her fondness for Jordan still lingered deep down, even though the man he was now wasn't the man he had been a few years earlier.

'He should be punished for what he's done to you,' Tor contradicted, his firm mouth compressing into a taut line.

'Mum *should* have left the house to both of us,' she protested on her brother's behalf. 'It must've been very hurtful for Jordan to realise that he'd been left out.'

'He wasn't her son, he was her stepson,' Tor pointed out drily. 'Generally parents do choose to leave their worldly goods to blood relatives.'

'And you think Jordan targeted me because I was left the house?' Pixie demanded angrily, jumping to her feet. 'Well, I think that's nonsense! Maybe he did cheat to get his hands on the money, but he cared about me.'

'I'm not saying that he didn't, but using you to get his hands on more money quickly became his main motivation. Before he got involved you had a secure future with the ownership of that house. Instead he ensured you were loaded down with mortgage payments and student loans,' Tor sliced in in a harsh undertone. 'And now some very dangerous men are chasing him for repayment, which puts both you and Alfie at risk. You *can't* go back to that house. You can't risk meeting up with Jordan in public again either.'

'You can't tell me that!' Pixie gasped. 'You can't tell me where I can live and what I can and can't do!'

'When it comes to your security I will tell you, particularly if it affects my son.'

'You didn't want to know about your son when I was pregnant last year!' Pixie slung at him vengefully. 'Don't expect me to have faith in you now!'

'You know now that I didn't remember you and that I'm only telling you what you don't want to hear because you need to know those facts,' Tor countered in his measured level drawl. 'But you *can* have faith in my determination to ensure that neither you nor my son are further affected by Jordan's bad choices.'

'But I *have* to go back to the house… I've got a cat to look after…and then there's all my stuff.' Pixie gasped, the ramifications of what he was telling her finally beginning to sink in.

'I'll make arrangements for you to remove your cat and your possessions immediately. There's a good chance that your brother's creditors will ransack the property and take anything that they can sell.'

Pixie went pale and broke out in nervous perspiration. 'Oh…my…word,' she whispered in horror. 'This is a nightmare.'

'With my support it doesn't have to be.' Tor pulled his phone out and began to make calls while she stared at him wordlessly.

He was on the phone for about ten minutes and it sounded as though he was rattling off instructions to someone. 'When you go to the house you will take my security team with you to protect you and you will leave Alfie here.'

Slowly, painfully, it was dawning on Pixie that, faced with impending homelessness, she was in no position to call any shots. 'But I can't move in here!' she exclaimed.

'I am more than happy to have you and Alfie here.'

'Well, possibly for a few days until I can move on. I'll have to find somewhere I can rent. Maybe there's someone at work I can share with. Thank goodness I'm not due back at work until next week,' she gabbled, covering her clammy face with her spread hands in an expression of near desperation as the true meaning of her position hit her hard.

'I'd prefer for you to stay on here,' Tor admitted. 'It will make it easier for me to get to know Alfie.'

'That's important to you, is it?'

'The most crucial thing in my life right now,'

Tor disconcerted her by declaring. 'I can't begin to tell you how much his existence matters to me.'

And Pixie almost scoffed at that turnaround in attitude on his part until she recalled the man with the haunted eyes telling her about his daughter's death, and she compressed her lips and said nothing, shame silencing her because she recognised sincerity when she saw it. Tor had only needed confirmation that Alfie was his to develop a serious interest in his son.

'You and I have had a very troubled start…but we don't have to continue in the same vein,' Tor framed almost roughly.

'We don't,' she agreed, welded to his beautiful eyes, bronzed by golden highlights and strong emotion.

'In time I genuinely believe that we could make something of this…attraction between us, potentially even marriage,' Tor spelt out almost curtly, so tough did he find it to broach the concept of a new relationship, particularly when he had promised himself that never again would he make such an attempt with a woman.

Pixie flushed and froze, not quite sure she had heard those words but keen to nip any such toxic notion in the bud. 'Oh, no…you and me? We're *not* going there,' she told him without hesitation.

His fine ebony brows drew together. He was not vain, but he was confident and arrogant, and he knew his own worth. He was richer than sin, reasonably good-looking and most women loved him. He wasn't remotely prepared for Pixie's blunt and woundingly *instant* rejection. 'Why not?' he asked equally bluntly.

A strangled laugh that was not one of amusement was wrenched from Pixie. She stared back at him wide-eyed, as if his proposition had been shocking.

'*Why not?* How can you ask me that?' she exclaimed. 'Five years after you lost your unfaithful wife you're *still* not over her and you're *still* wearing your wedding ring. No woman in her right mind would risk getting involved with you!'

For once in his life, Tor was silenced because it was a direct strike he hadn't been expecting. His ultimate goal was to marry Pixie and legitimise his son's birth and he had expected to proceed to that desirable conclusion by easy stages; the possibility of rejection had not once crossed his mind. Now it dawned on him that he could well be facing a long and stony road, toiling uphill every step of the way, because this was a woman who knew stuff no other woman had ever known about him and there would be no fooling her, no fobbing her off with something less than she felt she deserved.

'So, to sum up, you and me…well, you bury that idea,' Pixie advised him briskly. 'You and Alfie? Speed ahead…and I'll stay here until I get sorted out.'

It was a tragedy that he was so emotionally unavailable, so wrapped up in the past, she acknowledged unhappily. Marriage to Tor would have changed her life and Alfie's out of recognition but marrying a man still unhealthily attached to a past love would be a daily punishment for her. She could still remember the love between her parents and their relationship had struck her as a shining example of what marriage should be. She cringed at the prospect of being Tor's second-best and the likelihood that she would always be compared to her predecessor, whom he had loved. No, she had made the right decision, putting her own need for security and happiness above her son's needs...*hadn't she?*

CHAPTER SIX

IT WAS THE middle of the night or at least the early hours of the morning, Pixie guessed, when Tor shook her awake.

'Your brother's in hospital,' he told her grittily.

Pixie forced herself up on her elbows, shaken out of a sound sleep, and stared up at Tor, fully dressed and formidable. 'He's...*what*?'

'He's been beaten up by his creditors,' Tor divulged thinly. 'I wasn't sure whether or not to tell you.'

Pixie searched his lean dark features in wonderment. 'Of course, you tell me,' she protested. 'He's my brother and he screwed up, but I still love him!'

That bold statement of affection seemed to unnerve Tor slightly. His shimmering golden eyes hooded and cloaked as if she was showing him a softness that he didn't want to see in her. 'Does that mean that you want to see him?'

'Of course, I do,' she confirmed, clambering out

of bed, suddenly uneasily conscious of the reality that she was only clad in pyjamas and of how incredibly uncomfortable Tor could make her feel when she was anything less than fully dressed.

In recent nights, she had encountered Tor in the nursery when teething was making Alfie fractious and unwilling to settle and he would cry and cry. She usually told Emma to go back to bed and that she would take care of her son, but Tor had proved to be surprisingly invested in Alfie being upset, persisting with his presence when she had expected him to lose patience and leave them alone. And gradually, it had dawned on her that Tor was a father prepared to take the rough with the smooth and willing to help out when Alfie was less than his cheerful smiling self. Was that the result of his previous experience with young children or simply his drive to make up for that poor start in fatherhood that he had acknowledged? Whichever, Pixie was unwillingly impressed by Tor's ability to cope with his son even when he was whiny and miserable. Add in the reality that Tor was half-naked during those encounters, clad, as he was, in only a pair of faded jeans, and she was a woman, heaven forgive her for that truth, but suddenly she was fully on board with him pushing in where before she had had nobody but herself to depend on.

There was Tor, a six-pack of impressive musculature on parade, all bronzed and lethally built and sensual. With that temptation before her, being got out of bed in the middle of the night had, without warning, become a thrilling kind of adventure. She had to struggle to keep her attention on Alfie when Tor was there, bare-chested and sleepy, those gorgeous eyes drowsy and somehow even more compelling, the black spiky lashes strikingly noticeable and his eyes on her. Hot, hungry, interested. But she wasn't stupid and she wasn't going there—wasn't going to make that mistake *again*.

She was a pushover for Tor, she reckoned unhappily. One hint that he wanted something more and she was ready to jump on the chance. But that would only complicate things between them, she warned herself sagely. Tor was open to having sex with her, nothing more lasting, nothing deeper, she reckoned ruefully. She believed the idea of marrying her had been his knee-jerk conventional overreaction to the discovery that he was a father again, not a proposition that he was properly serious about. In the short term, however, Tor was a typical male, programmed to seek sexual satisfaction, and for the present he didn't seem to be seeking that outlet with any other woman, so she was convenient and available, but his apparent interest didn't mean anything more than that. It was wiser to keep her distance, retain her barriers and stay uninvolved while letting him build his relationship with Alfie separate from hers.

'A car will be waiting for you when you're ready.'

'You're not coming with me?' she heard herself say and reddened fiercely.

'I want to punch your brother too. He put you and Alfie in danger. You could've been in that house with him. You could've been hurt, and it would've been his fault,' Tor breathed rawly.

Pixie compressed her lips. It was several days since she had returned to the empty house and packed up their belongings and Coco. The move had been executed at frightening speed because Tor's aid had included a professional removal team and a van as well as a squad of Tor's security men to protect her. Within little more than an hour and a bit, everything she possessed had been transferred, much of it now stowed in an attic room on the top floor of the town house. Some day she would have to go through it all and she would probably dump a lot of what she had grabbed in haste, stuff that Jordan wouldn't value but she did. There had been the family photo albums, and her mother's treasured bits and pieces as well, items she would never part with, the objects that reminded her of her happy childhood and favourite moments, which she would, one day, share with Alfie.

'But Alfie and I have been with you, *safe*, and Jordan's my brother,' she muttered ruefully.

'Your *half*-brother,' Tor stressed.

'He was eight when I was born. He's been with

Get Up To 4 Free Books!

Dear Reader,

IT'S A FACT: if you answer 4 quick questions, we'll send you 4 FREE REWARDS from each series you try!

Try **Harlequin® Desire** books featuring the worlds of the American elite with juicy plot twists, delicious sensuality and intriguing scandal.

Try **Harlequin Presents®** Larger-Print books featuring the glamourous lives of royals and billionaires in a world of exotic locations, where passion knows no bounds.

Or **TRY BOTH!**

I'm not kidding you. As a leading publisher of women's fiction, we value your opinions... and your time. That's why we are prepared to reward you handsomely for completing our mini-survey. In fact, we have 4 Free Rewards for you, including 2 free books and 2 free gifts from each series you try!

Thank you for participating in our survey,

Pam Powers

To get your 4 FREE REWARDS:
Complete the survey below and return the insert today to receive up to 4 FREE BOOKS and FREE GIFTS guaranteed!

"4 for 4" MINI-SURVEY

1 Is reading one of your favorite hobbies?

☐ YES ☐ NO

2 Do you prefer to read instead of watch TV?

☐ YES ☐ NO

3 Do you read newspapers and magazines?

☐ YES ☐ NO

4 Do you enjoy trying new book series with FREE BOOKS?

☐ YES ☐ NO

Please send me my Free Rewards, consisting of **2 Free Books from each series I select** and **Free Mystery Gifts**. I understand that I am under no obligation to buy anything, as explained on the back of this card.

❏ **Harlequin Desire®** (225/326 HDL GQ3X)
❏ **Harlequin Presents® Larger-Print** (176/376 HDL GQ3X)
❏ **Try Both** (225/326 & 176/376 HDL GQ4A)

FIRST NAME   LAST NAME

ADDRESS

APT.#   CITY

STATE/PROV.   ZIP/POSTAL CODE

EMAIL ❏   Please check this box if you would like to receive newsletters and promotional emails from Harlequin Enterprises ULC and its affiliates. You can unsubscribe anytime.

HD/HP-520-MS20

me all my life. He might as well be my full brother,' Pixie countered steadily.

'A family connection isn't a forgive-all escape clause,' Tor objected, marvelling at her ongoing loyalty to a male who had let her down so badly. His half-brother, Sev, had betrayed him and Tor knew that he would never pardon him for his behaviour. Of course, his outlook had always been very black and white on such matters, he conceded, and clearly Pixie's was not.

And Pixie instantly knew that he was thinking of *his* brother, who had slept with his wife and whom he could not forgive.

'Jordan loves us. He's got nobody else,' Pixie stated almost apologetically in the face of Tor's disapproval. 'I need to be the bigger person here and try to help him.'

'Even if he's already burned all his boats?'

'He tried to tell me, warn me away to keep Alfie and me safe, but I think he was too ashamed to tell me the whole story.' Pixie sighed.

In spite of his attitude, Tor joined her in the waiting limo. It was barely dawn and the drive to the hospital was accomplished in silence. 'You don't need to do this,' she said awkwardly on the way in.

'If you're here, I'm here.'

Jordan was in a cubicle in A & E. He had been badly beaten, his face swollen, his eyes black. He had a broken arm and cracked ribs too and he

'Yes,' Pixie retorted tightly. 'And you can't have that in return because I'm not for sale and I'm not the sort of person who would trade sex for anything.'

Tor's self-discipline cracked and he grinned. 'I'm glad to hear that and I can work with what you've just told me.'

Pixie shot him an unconvinced glance. 'You... *can*?'

'I wouldn't want a woman who would use sex as a bargaining chip,' Tor traded smoothly. 'For the right price, I want *more* than sex.'

Pixie studied him in complete shock.

'You're so innocent. Why do you look so surprised?' Tor quipped. 'Virtually everything has a price.'

'Jordan's my family.'

'Who stole from you and put you and our son at risk of harm.'

'What did you mean about "the right price"?'

'My terms would be simple. That you agree to visit Greece with me to introduce Alfie to my family and consider marrying me.'

'Marrying you?' She gasped incredulously.

'You only have to consider the idea. When I first broached the idea, after all, you dismissed it without even considering it. I'm not going to try and force you into anything,' Tor proclaimed defensively. 'But I do want my family to meet Alfie.'

'I have to go back to work tomorrow.'

'Give me that trip to Greece and you'll never have to work again,' Tor murmured sibilantly. 'Seriously, the world will become your oyster.'

Breathless, Pixie whispered, 'And Jordan?'

'He gets therapy and a new start, but he has to be in the mindset to change, otherwise, I warn you, you're wasting your time,' he warned her flatly.

'I want him to have that chance…'

'Marry me and we'll be a family,' Tor told her.

And it was the perfect promise because Pixie longed to be part of a family again more than she wanted anything else. Jordan's deception had hit her hard and, while she still regarded her brother as family, he was now somewhere on the outside of that charmed circle until he could prove himself decent again.

'OK .. I'll go to Greece with you for a visit and I'll apply for unpaid leave from my job. I don't want to just give it up. I *like* working,' she admitted, while scarcely able to credit that she was willing to take that leap of faith into the unknown with him.

But her world and its boundaries had changed irrevocably, she acknowledged ruefully. She could no longer trust Jordan because, clearly, he was addicted to gambling. He had stolen her inheritance from her, frittered away her hard-earned cash, destroyed her trust. Even if Jordan recovered, it could be years before she could have faith in him again because addiction was a slippery slope and he would always be fighting temptation. And Jordan had put both her and Alfie at risk. Tor, at the very least, was keen to put Alfie's best interests first, and that Tor was keen to introduce their son to his family impressed her. He could've kept Alfie as a dark little secret and visited him discreetly and nobody would ever have known that the little boy existed.

Instead, Tor had chosen to be open and honest with his relatives and he was making room for his son everywhere in his life. Only, what did that mean for her? Not marriage, she couldn't marry a man simply because he had got her pregnant, could she? But everything in her once stable world was shifting, she conceded apprehensively, and it was happening so fast that it left her breathless.

'You and Alfie will need new clothes. It's much warmer out there,' Tor completed. 'A shopping trip is on the cards.'

But Pixie was still thinking over his insistence that she consider marrying him. She had noticed that he had finally removed his wedding ring but naturally she hadn't said anything about it. 'Why do you want me to consider marrying you?' she asked bluntly.

'Two parents would be better than one for Alfie. I want him to have my name and my family, to become part of that support system. I want to be fully involved in his upbringing, not standing on the sidelines. Without taking him away from you, I want to share him,' he delineated tautly. 'But that's all for him and me. For us—well, we'd be a work in progress but we'd be a family and the attraction between us is strong.'

'I would need love.'

'I have to be honest. I don't think I could do love again.'

'Because you're scared,' Pixie breathed in a softer tone of understanding.

'It's nothing to do with fear,' Tor asserted between gritted teeth of repudiation, insulted by that interpretation of his natural reservations. 'I grew up with Katerina. She was my first love. I was young, naïve and idealistic. I'm not that boy any more. I'm a man and my expectations of a woman are much more practical and prosaic. You have abilities that I respect and value. Loyalty to your brother, in spite of the fact that he's let you down badly. You have compassion for the weak because, make no mistake, Jordan *is* weaker than you and in trying to help him you could be setting yourself up for a world of hurt and disappointment.'

'I'm willing to take that chance and, even though some of what you've said makes sense, I'd want more than practicality in marriage. I'd want passion.'

'I can give you passion,' Tor told her boldly, shimmering eyes welded to hers, and all the oxygen in the car suddenly seemed to be sucked up. 'I can give you as much passion as you can handle.'

'Passion *and* love from a guy who's willing to take a risk on me.'

'Successful bankers estimate the risks they take in advance and without emotion getting involved.'

Pixie nodded in acceptance and sighed. 'I'm not a cold person.'

'No, you're not…and my family are not cold either. For Alfie's sake, I'm glad you are the way you are, but that doesn't change the fact that you and I are very different. We would only work as a couple if you could accept those differences.'

'I'd always be wanting more,' Pixie told him, wondering why her eyes were prickling and stinging, why she suddenly felt all worked up about a perfectly innocent and unthreatening conversation. Aside of that sexual sizzle between them, they didn't suit and that was that—better by far to see and accept that now than try to fight it. So, Katerina had been his first love, his *only* love, which was probably why her treachery had been so massively damaging. After all, if he couldn't trust the girl he had grown up with, who could he trust?

'I have every hope that you'll change your mind,' Tor murmured. 'Should I have lied and said that I could give you what you want?'

'You can't fake emotion. I'd have seen through you.'

'Most people can't read me.'

'I saw you at your lowest. You have certain tells,' she told him gently, thinking of his body language that night when Alfie had been conceived: the haunted dark eyes, his lean, restless hands shifting with the grace and eloquence that were so much a part of him, the emotion that seethed inside him, the emotion that he denied and suppressed.

Tor elevated a fine ebony brow. 'We're definitely going to have to discuss the tells.'

Emerging from that disturbing recollection of their first meeting, Pixie went pink, trembling a little as that unavoidable flood of physical awareness shifted like melted honey down deep inside her, warming her from the inside out as she pressed her thighs together and stiffened defensively. She wanted to slap herself for even those few moments of remembrance, for an indulgence she no longer allowed herself. To maintain boundaries, she too needed to put that intimate past knowledge of Tor behind her.

'No, we're not arguing about this any longer…you are *not* buying me clothes!' Pixie told Tor heatedly. 'You can pay for Alfie's clothes, but *not mine*.'

'Have you any idea how much money I must owe you in terms of child support?' Tor enquired calmly.

And it was precisely that calm and lack of embarrassment that riled Pixie. She didn't want to discuss money with Tor. She didn't want to admit that she was pretty much broke because she'd never had sufficient cash to manage to save. Paying what she had believed to be her share of the mortgage and buying food every month had cleaned her out and reduced her wardrobe to 'must-have' slender proportions.

She had forgotten what it felt like to buy something just because she liked it or fancied something new because, nine times out of ten, Alfie had needed something more. And now Tor was trying to hand her credit cards, open accounts for her, put her in the hands of some fancy stylist so that she could do him proud in Greece, and it was all too much for her to handle. Registering that she was on the brink of silly tears because he wasn't listening to her, Pixie pushed her trembling hands down on the arms of her chair and stood up.

'I can't listen to any more of this… I'm out,' she said thinly, and walked out of the dining room.

Tor released his breath in a groan and drained his wine glass, pushing away the plate in front of him because his appetite had died. For long minutes he sat and pondered his dilemma. How was she planning to buy clothes without money? Why was she so resistant to his financial help when it came to her personal needs? Had he ever even heard of a woman refusing a new wardrobe before?

When the table was being cleared, and after he had politely refused his housekeeper's suggestion

that she make something else for him to eat, Tor
vaulted upright and followed Pixie upstairs. There
was nothing more frustrating than someone who
walked away from a dispute, he registered in frustration, although he could not recall *ever* having an
argument with a woman before the night on which
Katerina had died. He and Katerina had never argued prior to that, had had no differences of opinion, minor or major. In essence they had not talked
that much. Maybe those had been revealing signs
of an unhealthy or, at the very least, boring relationship, he conceded grimly. How did he know?
He hadn't had a single relationship since then and
if he had ever had any skills in that field, they had
to be distinctly rusty.

He knocked on her bedroom door and scowled.
That was another problem: the whole 'separate bedrooms' thing was tying him up in knots. Why did
she make such a big deal of sex? Sex was physical,
not a pursuit anyone needed to imbue with magical
properties or meaning. Was it because the only time
she had indulged in sex she had ended up pregnant?
Or could she simply be resistant to his advances because that one-off experience with him had been
lousy? That drunk, how considerate could he have
been? Tor clenched his teeth together and wondered
if he could bring himself to ask. He knocked again.
He *needed* to know, he *needed* details. He recalled
sufficiently to be aware that he had enjoyed himself

thoroughly, but that did not mean that his partner had also enjoyed the experience.

'What?' Pixie demanded aggressively as she flung the door wide on him. Dragged out of the shower by the knocking on the door, she was in a thoroughly bad mood.

There she was, not even five feet tall and barefoot and wrapped in a stupid towel, which covered her delectable curves from neck to toe. Why did his housekeeper buy such *huge* towels in his household? Tor wondered absently. And why did the angry fire of challenge in Pixie's bright blue eyes turn him on?

'We need to talk.'

'No, we don't,' Pixie argued, trying to close the door on him.

'Yes, we *do*,' Tor decreed, stalking over the threshold, automatically gathering her up into his arms, a warm, struggling, fragrant bundle of damp femininity that fiercely aroused him. He was shocked by that reaction as he carefully laid her back down on the bed. 'You explain to me now why you won't allow me to buy you clothes when you need them…'

'Where's your furry loincloth? You're behaving like a guy who just walked out of a Stone Age cave!' Pixie snapped back at him.

'I need to understand the problem before I can fix it,' Tor breathed in a raw undertone.

'I don't need you to fix *everything* in my life,'

Pixie muttered. 'I mean, you've already spent a fortune trying to sort out Jordan. Isn't that enough?'

'That was our agreement and I haven't spent a fortune. You wouldn't let me buy the house for him.'

'No, because that would have cost too much and Jordan needs to rebuild his life somewhere new,' Pixie reasoned. 'He has to become self-sufficient again and he shouldn't be rewarded for what he's done. You don't need *all* of us hanging on your sleeve like scroungers.'

Tor gave up the ghost and groaned out loud in frustration, sinking down on the edge of the bed and raking impatient fingers through his cropped black hair 'Why would you think for one moment that I would look on the mother of my child as a scrounger? Have I done or said anything to give you that impression?'

'Well, no,' she conceded grudgingly. 'But it's how I feel… Why is the clothes thing so important to you?'

'I want you to feel comfortable with my family and friends. I don't want you to feel inappropriately dressed or out of place.'

'Are you afraid my appearance is going to embarrass you?' she whispered, thinking that if she flew out with her well-worn winter wardrobe there was a good chance that it would, and that there was an even stronger chance that she might be mistaken for one of the cleaners that came into the town house to clean several times a week. And that would definitely embarrass everybody, not just her. He was winning the argument, she thought ruefully—he was winning without even trying.

Tor closed a large hand over hers. 'Nothing you could do would embarrass me. I'm thinking of your comfort, your ability to relax.'

'Maybe it would help if you told me about where you're taking me.'

'An island called Milnos. I bought it a few years ago. The property I built is large enough to house my family when they come to visit. They live on Corfu. One of my brothers, Kristo, is still at school. Dimitri is at university and the eldest, Nikolaos, works for my father in his shipping company.'

'No sisters?'

'None. And so far I'm the only son who has married. Sofia was my parents' first grandchild and her death hit my family as hard as it hit me,' Tor confided tautly, trying to ignore the small fingers gently smoothing over his thigh in a gesture that he knew was intended to offer comfort but which was, instead, travelling straight to his groin and winding him up. 'That's why I want them to meet Alfie. My family are overdue for a glimpse of a brighter future.'

'Yes, I'm pretty sure you haven't been a bundle of laughs to be around,' Pixie mumbled, and then flushed at having made that tactless comment. 'Sorry—'

Tor grinned down at her, relishing the flushed triangle of her animated face beneath the tousled curls. 'You could be right... I've been all about work and nothing else for a long time, but I'm lighter-hearted around you...when we're not arguing, of course.'

'OK. I'll see the stylist and pick clothes,' Pixie muttered with a slight grimace. 'But I'd much prefer not to have to let you pay.'

Tor stared down at her, dark golden eyes unashamedly hungry. 'Do you think you could include some sexy underthings in the selection?' he murmured thickly.

Her cheeks burned. 'What would be the point?'

'My imagination thrives on fuel,' Tor husked, bending down slowly.

Her fingers skimmed up from his wide shoulders into his luxuriant black hair. He smelt amazing to her, fresh and earthy and male, a faint hint of citrus fruit in his designer cologne, that scent achingly familiar to her, achingly evocative. It was the same cologne he had worn *that* night. Her brain was telling her with increasing urgency to push him away, to sit up, to *stop* touching him, but her body was rebelling against common sense with Tor that close. She could feel the heat of his big body through the towel she was wrapped in, the stinging sensation of her nipples snapping taut, the warm damp ache making her feel hollow between her thighs. Every nerve ending was sitting up and taking screaming notice. It was like a wave of physical insanity taking her over.

'I like your fingers on me,' Tor muttered raggedly as he lowered his mouth to hers, let those sensual lips play across hers in a wildly arousing fashion that brought her out in a fever of awareness and damp heat. 'I'd like them all over me, your mouth as well—'

'We said we weren't doing this.'

'*You* said. I didn't make any promises,' Tor said urgently against her parted lips before his tongue delved between, and suddenly speech of any kind was beyond her. And she was bargaining shamelessly with herself: a few kisses. Where was the harm in that? And he was such an amazing kisser, it would be foolish to deny herself the experience.

Her hand slid off his thigh over his crotch, tracing the hard thrust of his erection, and he shuddered against her, his mouth hotter and harder than ever on hers, and she wanted nothing so much as for him to whip off the towel, lay her back and sate the unbearable longing as he had once before. She wanted him and he wanted her, no denying that. But when it went wrong, she thought frantically, Alfie would be caught up in the fallout and her relationship with Tor would become fatally toxic. Having sex with Tor again would come with a price tag attached and a series of risks. One or both of them would ultimately be disappointed and that would lead to discord.

'We can't do this,' she groaned against the urgency of his mouth.

'I can do this fine,' Tor contradicted.

And discomfiture washed over her because she had encouraged him, given him expectations, and she didn't like to be provocative. 'You shouldn't touch me,' she told him.

'You shouldn't touch me either.'

Her face burned so hot she was afraid that she would spontaneously combust. 'I'm acting like a tease and that's not me.'

'No, you need time to decide what you want and I'm not giving you space the way I promised because you're too damn tempting,' Tor growled, setting her back from him, scorching golden eyes smouldering over her discomfited face. 'I'm just naturally impatient and assertive when I want something. You need to push back hard to handle me when I get too enthusiastic.'

'But how does that work when I'm enthusiastic too?'

'You marry me,' Tor said simply.

CHAPTER SEVEN

'NOT WITHOUT LOVE,' Pixie protested.

'I've got lust covered,' Tor said almost insouci-
antly as he reclined back on her bed, completely
unashamed of the arousal tenting his tailored trousers. 'I've got lust in spades.'

And Pixie thought about it in that moment—
seriously thought about marrying a man because
she couldn't keep her hands off him—until all her
common sense stood up and screamed at her to get
her brain back in gear.

'We need more,' she told him heavily.

'We've got Alfie, and Alfie will benefit from
having an equal share of both of us. Two parents
together, *united*.'

'You're still hung up on Katerina.'

'No. I've taken the ring off. That's behind me. I
can't promise love because that's an emotional state
and I don't know if I'm capable of feeling like that

again,' Tor told her frankly. 'But I can tell you that I'll be faithful and trustworthy and secure.'

And she wanted him, dear heaven, Pixie had never wanted anything as she wanted Tor at that moment because she saw that he was willing to try, she saw that he had moved himself on, indeed that the eruption of her and Alfie into his life had fundamentally changed his outlook. But was it enough?

'I'd be taking a chance on you...and I don't do that,' she whispered honestly. 'I always play safe.'

'I'll *make* it work. You marry me and I'll make it work,' Tor intoned fiercely. 'We can be married within a couple of days and you can meet my family as my wife.'

And that offer had undeniable power because she had naturally been nervous of meeting his family. Being a wife would give her more status than merely being his illegitimate son's mother, a position that would only leave his family questioning exactly what their relationship encompassed. If she went to Greece with him, the two of them would be very much under scrutiny, which made her uneasy. She had watched Tor with Alfie, watched him being patient and caring. She could look for no more than that in the father of her son.

Even though it had gone against the grain, Tor had extended a helping hand to Jordan because that was what *she* wanted him to do. Even if she only married him for Alfie's sake and security, she would be making the right choice, she reasoned. But that wouldn't be the only reason she married him, her conscience piped up, and her face heated. She could have him in bed, if she married him, no worries about what he might think of her for succumbing, no worries about where that intimacy could be heading because marriage would give them the solid framework that they lacked.

Pixie breathed in deep and fast. 'OK... I'll marry you, so that we can be a real family.'

Tor lowered lush black lashes over stunned eyes at that seemingly snap decision, wondering what he had said right, *done* right to ultimately convince her round to his point of view. 'I'll get it organised.'

Pixie nodded slowly. 'I want a proper wedding though,' she warned him. 'I know you've already done it before, but this is my first time.'

'*Last* time,' he qualified. 'And I understand. If you have no objection, my mother will be ecstatic to be asked to organise a wedding reception and we'll get married in Greece.'

'You're looking for trouble,' Eloise pronounced after Pixie had finished breathlessly sharing her insecurities on the topic of marrying Tor. 'Why are you doing that?'

Pixie's smooth brow furrowed as yet another model strolled out wearing a dream wedding dress, only unfortunately, not one she had seen so far matched *her* dream. She lacked the height and shape to do puffy or elaborate or dramatic. But concentrating even on something as superficial as choosing her wedding gown was a challenge when her brain was eaten up by so many other worries.

'Am I?'

'Yes,' Eloise confirmed without hesitation. 'Tor is hotter than sin and richer than an oil well. So, he comes with some baggage like a first wife he may not be over... Well, who *doesn't* have baggage? Start appreciating what you've got, Pixie. Even if he gets bored and dumps you a few years down the road, you'll be left financially secure and Alfie will still have his father. You can't expect to get a man like Tor, a wedding ring and undying love too. Life isn't a fairy tale.'

'I know it's not, but do you think he can be faithful?' Pixie whispered. 'I mean, from everything I've read online about him, he's been quite a womaniser.'

'I think if Tor plays away, he's clever enough to be discreet and you'll never know about it,' Eloise countered cynically. 'And I know that's not what you want to hear but if you can content yourself with what you've got you'll be far happier.'

Pixie swallowed hard, well aware that the brunette was not the person to turn to for reassurance because Eloise had been hurt and disappointed by men too many times. She was a good friend, but she always spoke her mind and she was correct—she had yet to say anything that Pixie had wanted to hear. Eloise had already pointed out that she was boxing above her weight with Tor, that she had landed the equivalent of a super tanker when by rights on the strength of her attractions she had only been due a tugboat. Pixie hadn't needed those reminders of her own essential insignificance, her ordinariness and her lack of any surpassing beauty or talent.

Perhaps unwisely, she had researched Tor's first wife online and had read about the tragic accident that had occurred at their London home, which had later been sold. And she had seen what Katerina looked like: a truly beautiful slender brunette with almond-shaped dark eyes and a mane of dark, glossy hair. She had been on board a yacht, her wonderful hair blowing, looking all athletic and perfect and popular with a bunch of friends around her. After that first glimpse, something inside Pixie had died along with curiosity and she had looked for no further photos.

Tor was in Brussels attending a banking conference and Pixie had been kitting herself out with a new wardrobe and her wedding gown. In the end she had only invited three people to the Greek wedding, Eloise and a couple of gay friends, male nurses she had trained with, who had accompanied her to the stylist and laughed her out of her attempts to go light on Tor's wallet. Jordan had refused to come to Greece, which had hurt, but at the same time she had understood that, in his current mood as he underwent counselling for his addiction and was forced to face all his mistakes, the idea of having to put on a front for strangers at her wedding was more than he could bear. Tor's comments on the same score had, predictably, been a good deal more critical.

Pixie had also had to find and engage a new nanny because Emma was only temporary and preferred moving between different jobs. Actually, having to interview potential employees had been nerve-racking for her, but Tor had pointed out quite rightly on the phone that she wouldn't be happy leaving the task to him. She had found Isla, a cheerful young Scot, who had struck up an instant connection with Alfie that impressed her and who couldn't wait to make a trip to Greece.

'Oh, that's *it*,' Pixie said warmly, focusing appreciatively on the slender sheath dress with the pretty scalloped neckline that the current model was displaying. 'That's definitely the dress.'

'But it's very plain. A bride needs more pizzazz,' Eloise opined in surprise at the choice.

'It's got enough pizzazz for me.' Pixie laughed, knowing that the dress probably cost a small fortune even though it was unadorned, because they were in a designer bridal salon.

'Don't you think you should go for something fancier for a big society wedding?' Eloise made one last attempt to sway her.

'No, it's not going to be a large event. Tor said it would be small and it's my day and I'm not going to worry about trying to impress people.' *As if she could*, she was thinking ruefully, having decided that the only sensible way to behave was to be herself without any false airs or graces.

Three days later, Pixie flew out of London with her friends and Alfie and Isla on board Tor's private jet. It was her wedding day and all she had to do was show up with her dress and a magic wand would take care of all the other necessities—at least according to Tor, that was. In reality, she was pretty apprehensive about what was coming next. They landed in Athens to VIP treatment and they were ushered straight onto a helicopter to complete the journey to Milnos. She had her friends to comment out loud on the luxury and ease of their journey and what life was like on the five-star side of the fence. And all she could think, thoroughly intimidated as she was by the champagne offered on boarding by attractive stewardesses and the constant service, was how on earth was she ever going to fit into this new world where wealth provided so many of the extras she had never enjoyed before?

For that reason, arriving in the lush landscaped grounds of the Sarantos property on the island, a

massive white villa with wings radiating out from
it, and meeting up with her future in-laws came
as a huge relief. Pandora Sarantos was reassuringly motherly and friendly, and she lit up like a
firework display the instant she laid eyes on Alfie.
Alfie suddenly became the eighth wonder of the
world and Pixie could not be uncomfortable with
an older woman that keen to admire and appreciate
her son. By her side, Hallas, a shorter, greying version of his sons, was less vocal but truly welcoming.
He apologised for the absence of his younger sons,
who were with Tor, he explained, and he asked if
he could have the honour of walking her down the
aisle. Pixie agreed, pleased not to have to undergo
the stress of having to walk that aisle alone in front
of strangers and touched by the offer, a pang of pain
arrowing through her as she thought how much her
father would have enjoyed fulfilling that role for
her. It would have been wonderful to have her parents with her to share the day, she conceded, but
Tor's parents were a comfort and their enthusiasm
for Alfie was very welcome.

'Alfie is so beautiful, with your hair and Tor's
eyes,' Pandora enthused in fluent English as Alfie
tottered upright, gripping the edge of a metallic
coffee table in the foyer. 'Tor will have to tackle
childproofing everything here. Let me show you
up to the nursery...'

As Pixie left her friends being shown to their

rooms with wide eyes fixed to their palatial surroundings, she followed Pandora Sarantos upstairs
with Alfie and the nanny, Isla.

'Wow, this is some place,' the nanny remarked
in a shaken undertone.

Pixie was relieved to have someone else comment on the sheer splendour of the marble stairs
and hallways and the airy grandeur of the sunlit
walkways left open to balconies and fabulous island and sea views.

'This is *your* home now,' Tor's mother announced, disconcerting Pixie. 'I may be here to
host your wedding but I'm not the interfering type.
I won't be visiting without invitation or anything
of that nature. Tor's father, Hallas, and I are really
happy that Tor is settling down again.'

Because that's the agreement, Pixie reflected,
thinking that she and Tor really were going to have
a marriage based on the most practical rules. He
would settle down in order to gain regular access
to his son and have Alfie become a Sarantos by
name. Alfie's mother, Tor's bride, was more or less
an afterthought, a necessary step towards reaching those all-important goals. Clearly, Tor's chatty
mother had assumed that their marriage was of a
more personal, normal nature and she could hardly
be blamed for that when most couples married because they were in love with each other, Pixie reasoned ruefully.

Pandora spread open the door of a room furnished as a nursery but not the usual nursery, Pixie adjusted, scanning in wonderment shelves of new toys and every luxury addition known to early childhood. It was a nursery arranged for a little prince, not a normal toddler. 'I can't tell you what a thrill I had furnishing this room for Alfie,' the older woman explained volubly. 'I was so excited to find out about him and you and Tor. You and Alfie are exactly what I was hoping would arrive in his life…a new family.'

And you couldn't get much more of a welcome mat than that, Pixie conceded, warmed to the heart by that little speech and finally appreciating, as her soon-to-be mother-in-law looked yearningly at Alfie and smiled, that her son was so welcome and that she was equally welcome because obviously Tor's parents had assumed that he had fallen in love again. Any parents that loved their son and had seen him heartbroken by the tragic end to his first marriage would want to see him embark on a fresh relationship. Yet even they didn't know the truth of how very tragic and soul-destroying that prior marriage had been for Tor, she acknowledged ruefully, because they didn't know about the infidelity and heartbreak involved.

'I mustn't keep you back from your bridal beautifying,' the older woman remarked with a sudden smile. 'It's a wonderfully exciting day for all of us.'

'She's lovely,' Pixie told Eloise when she arrived in the suite of rooms designated as the bridal suite.

'"Mothers-in-law" and "lovely" don't go together in the same sentence,' Eloise told her in dismay at the statement. 'There's probably a hidden agenda there and it'll take time for you to work it out.'

'I don't think that's true this time,' Pixie said with assurance, because she had recognised the genuine warmth in Tor's mother. 'Wait until you meet her properly. I think she's just happy that her son has found someone and that there's a grand-child. Alfie's going to be spoilt rotten.'

A pair of strangers entered, accompanied by a young, very pretty brunette, who seemed to be there to act as an interpreter and who introduced herself as Angelina Raptis, a friend of the family. One of her companions was a hairstylist, Pixie learned, and the other a make-up artist.

'I don't wear a lot of make-up,' Pixie began un-certainly.

'But today you *do*,' Eloise whispered in her ear. 'Today is special. You want to look your very best and feel good.'

Pixie acquiesced, wanting to at least fit nomi-nally with Tor's expectations. The stylist wanted to cut and straighten her hair and she mustered the courage to say that she preferred her curls and sim-ply wanted to wear her hair up in some fashion.

'I love curls. They're *so* natural,' Angelina commented. 'How brave of you to leave them like that for a formal occasion.'

Encountering the steely glint in the brunette's eyes and noting the scornful curve of her lips, Pixie reddened and turned her head away again, recognising that Angelina was a bit of a shrew while conceding that she couldn't expect everyone she met at her wedding to be a genuine friendly well-wisher.

'I can't wait to meet your son,' Angelina told her brightly. 'Does he look like Tor?'

'Yes, although he's fair-haired like me. He has Tor's eyes though.'

'A very handsome little boy, then. I admire you for being so calm.'

In the background, Eloise was grimacing but, mercifully, her other friends Denny and Steve had come in to join the bridal preparation team and lighten the mood.

'Pixie's looking forward to enjoying a wonderful day,' Denny said cheerfully, earning a relieved smile from Pixie, who loved his positive attitude.

'Even with that awful story in the press?' Angelina burbled, startling Pixie. 'I really admire your strength, Pixie.'

'What press? What awful story?' Pixie repeated in consternation. 'What are you referring to?'

Denny groaned out loud while Eloise stared at Angelina as though she wanted to strangle her where she stood. 'Until you spoke up, we were keeping that story to ourselves, flower,' Denny told Angelina.

'What story?' Pixie whispered afresh, her heart sinking although she had done nothing that she knew that she should be ashamed of.

'Some viper called Saffron sold a story to a tabloid newspaper about the night you met Tor,' Steve explained. 'And the newspaper did a little digging and made a fluffy story out of it.'

Saffron—the wannabe actress who had brought Tor back to that house Pixie had temporarily stayed in; Saffron, the redhead he had rejected and a woman who would probably relish publicity exposure. What on earth could she have to say about anything? Had she seen Tor leaving the bedroom the next morning? That was the only explanation, Pixie decided unhappily.

'Let me see it,' she said to Denny, who was already tapping his phone.

'I'm so sorry. I didn't mean to upset anyone,' Angelina said plaintively.

'You don't dump that sort of stuff on a bride,' Steve said stiffly.

'I'm sure you didn't mean anything by it,' Pixie said politely, forgivingly, her heart racing until Denny had handed her his phone and she glimpsed a very glamorous photo of Saffron next to a brief article about the billionaire banker about to marry the nurse he had got pregnant on a one-night stand.

News of her pregnancy had probably got back to Saffron by way of her housemate, Steph, who had given Pixie her cat, Coco. Steph was also the sister of one of Pixie's former colleagues. A stray piece of gossip had probably exposed Pixie's secret pregnancy, she thought heavily, and Saffron had put two and two together to register that they made a very neat four.

'Then I suppose that I shouldn't say that Tor is absolutely furious,' Angelina revealed. 'Look, I feel awkward now… I'll leave you to get dressed with your friends.'

'And you'll not be making a friend of that toxic piece,' Eloise breathed wrathfully.

'If there's nothing untrue in the article I'll just have to live with it,' Pixie pronounced with a stiff smile as she struggled to conceal how mortified she was that Tor's family and friends should have access to the bare shameless facts of their first meeting. 'Let's just forget about it for now.'

'Why on earth would Tor be furious?' Eloise scoffed.

'Because I expect he likes his private life to stay private, like me.' Pixie sighed as the make-up artist fluttered around her, one soft brush after another tickling her brow bone and her cheeks and every other part of her face.

'You're going to look totally amazing,' Eloise told her bracingly.

Denny gave her a fond appraisal. 'A complete princess…'

'A trophy bride,' Steve completed, not to be out-done on the soothing-compliment front.

After presenting her with a beautiful bouquet of roses, Hallas Sarantos accompanied her down to the church in the village down by the harbour. They travelled in a flower-bedecked vintage car that he confided belonged to him as he admitted to a passion for classic cars. Pixie thanked him for all that he and his wife had done to make the wed-ding possible, and then she was stepping out with a smile into the warmth and brightness of the day outside the small village church. Her smile lurched a little when she saw how packed the church was and the sea of faces that turned to look at her because being so much the centre of attention unnerved her.

Instead, she chose to gaze down the aisle at Tor and, reassuringly, he didn't look angry, only his usual cool self-possessed self. And so incredibly handsome that he stole her breath away at that mo-ment just as he had the very first time she saw him, her attention lingering on the slashing black sweep of his brows, the sculpted high cheekbones that lent his features that perfect definition, the straight nose and the masculine fullness of his sensual mouth. It was as if looking at him lit a whole row of little fires inside her, flushing her face with warmth, fill-

ing the more sensitive areas of her body with heat
and sexual awareness.

There was a smile in the stunning bronzed eyes
that met hers at the altar, no, not absolutely furious about anything, Pixie decided, liberated from
that apprehension. If he even knew about the newspaper piece, and she doubted that he did, it evidently
hadn't annoyed him in the slightest. He eased the
wedding ring over her knuckle and the ceremony
was complete. Tor had become her husband and she
was now his wife, a conclusion that still shook her.

'You look ravishing,' he murmured on the way
out of the church, dark eyes sliding over the shapely
silhouette that the elegant gown somehow accentu-
ated, noting the way the fine silk defined the lush
plumpness of her breasts and the full curve of her
derrière, and more than a little surprised to realise
that he was categorically aroused by the prospect
of taking his bride to bed, even though he *was* furious with her for the choices she had made. Bad
choices, wrong decisions, the sort of mistake he
had to expect from someone as youthful and inexperienced in the world as she was, he reminded
himself grimly.

'Your parents are brilliant,' she told him chirpily.
'You lucked out there. Neither one of them asked
me a single awkward question.'

'Wait until you meet my three brothers, none

of whom are known for their tact,' Tor parried
smoothly.

And the car swept them back to the enormous
villa, where a throng far larger than Pixie had an-
ticipated awaited them in a vast room with orna-
mental pillars that could only have been described
as a modern ballroom. 'You married someone who's
got a freaking ballroom!' Denny gasped in her ear.
'And his mother is *still* calling this affair "a very
small do"!'

Possibly by Sarantos standards it was small,
Pixie conceded as she was tugged inexorably into
a receiving line to meet their guests and the long
procession of names and faces quickly became a
blur. Personal friends, business acquaintances, family friends and relatives. Tor's three brothers were
remarkably like him in looks. There truly was a
very large number of people present and the only
light moment of the experience for Pixie was when
Isla appeared with her son and Alfie made a mad
scramble out of her arms to reach his mother, smiling and chattering nonsense. Dressed in the cutest
little miniature suit she had ever seen, Alfie was
overjoyed at the reunion and it was a shock to her
when, after giving her a hug, he twisted and held
out his arms to greet Tor as if it was the most natural thing in the world.

Her baby boy was growing up and there was
room in his little heart for a father now, and the

immediacy of Tor's charismatic smile and pleasure at that enthusiastic greeting from his son warmed Pixie as well. It was just at that moment that a tall dark man appeared in front of them and Tor froze, his grasp on Alfie tightening enough that the baby complained and squirmed in his hold.

'Pixie, this is my half-brother, Sevastiano Cantarelli... I didn't realise you were attending,' he said flatly.

'I was determined to drop in and offer my congratulations. I can't stay for long,' Sevastiano responded in his low-pitched drawl. 'It means a lot to Papa.'

'Yes, yes, it would.' Tor acknowledged with a razor-edged smile as the other man moved on past, as keen to be gone, it seemed, as Tor was to see him go.

'If you would simply tell your family the truth, you wouldn't have been put in the position of having to entertain him,' she whispered helplessly.

'Don't interfere in what you don't understand!' Tor countered with icy bite and she paled with hurt and surprise and looked away again, suddenly appreciating that she had spoken too freely on what was a controversial topic in Tor's life. He might have spilled his guts the night they first met, but alcohol had powered those revelations, she reminded herself doggedly. His reaction now was a disquietingly harsh reminder that she was *still* an outsider, a virtual newcomer in Tor's world, not someone who should have assumed that she had the right to wade in and offer an opinion on a matter that private and personal.

CHAPTER EIGHT

A PERFECTLY CATERED MEAL was served by uniformed staff. Speeches were made by some of Tor's relatives and he translated them for her.

'You're very quiet,' Tor murmured then. 'I was rude earlier. I'm sorry.'

'No, sometimes I have no filter and it was a sensitive subject.'

'Let me explain,' Tor urged, skating a fingertip across the back of her clenched fingers, letting her know that *he* knew that she was still as wound up as a clock by his rebuke. 'For various reasons, Sev didn't get to know our father until he had grown up and their relationship now means a lot to Hallas. My mother has become very fond of him as well. If I spoke up, it would tear them all apart. My father is a very moral man and he would feel he had to choose between his sons and exclude Sev. What good would that anguish and disappointment do any of us now?'

'Your attitude is generous.' Pixie was impressed by his unselfish, mature outlook while recognising the sense of family responsibility that he had allowed to trap him into silence. 'But if your family had understood what you were *really* going through back then, they might have been able to offer you better support.'

'All of that is behind me now,' Tor insisted with impressive conviction. 'Meeting you gave me something of a second chance.'

'No, Alfie did that,' Pixie contradicted without hesitation.

Tor gritted his teeth at that response but said nothing. Knowing that he was to blame for every low point in their relationship was a new experience for him and not one anyone could have said he enjoyed. His bride wasn't in love with him, didn't think he was the best thing ever to happen to her and didn't even particularly crave what he could buy her either. His rational mind argued with that appraisal, reminding him that Katerina's supposed love, which, ironically, he had never once doubted, had been an empty vessel. Love didn't need to have anything to do with his marriage. And Pixie was naïve, honest though, loyal, everything Katerina had not been. For the very first time, he mulled over the truth that Katerina had lied to him and conducted an affair with another man that had begun even before their marriage. Three years of lies including Sofia's birth, he reflected angrily, and even the anger was new because he was making comparisons and he saw now so clearly that his first marriage had been all wrong from the very outset.

So, this time around, Tor reflected grimly, he wasn't compromising, he wasn't making any allowances for misunderstandings or mistakes. He was going to be who he was, tough, and when it came to telling his wife that she had gone wrong he was going to grasp that hot iron and go for the burn.

'Where are we going?' Pixie questioned breathlessly some hours later as she climbed out of the car down at the small harbour. 'And what about Alfie?'

'Alfie and his nanny will join us tomorrow. We can manage one night without him…*right?*' Tor arrowed up a questioning black brow as he bent down, curving an arm to her spine, and even in moonlight she felt the heat of embarrassment at being exposed as an overprotective mother.

As her gaze clashed in the moonlight with those stunning dark glittering eyes of his, her heart jumped inside her chest and her lower limbs turned liquid. His fierce attraction rocked her where she stood and almost instinctively she leant into him for support, literally mortified by the effect he could have on her because the feelings he inspired in her were so powerful and so far removed, she believed, from his reaction to her.

'It would be cruel to lift Alfie out of his cot at this hour,' she agreed, deliberately stepping back a few inches from him, striving to act cooler.

'Especially after he was exhausted by his social whirl.' Tor's expressive mouth quirked as he recalled his son being passed around like a parcel between groups of cooing women during the reception. Alfie certainly wasn't shy, and his unusual combination of golden curls and dark eyes attracted attention as much as his smiles and chuckles. 'At least he wasn't scared and shaken up like he was the day Jordan abandoned him,' Tor completed, knowing he would never forget the sight of his son clawing his way up his mother's body and clinging in the aftermath of an ordeal that had visibly traumatised him.

Pixie gasped a little in surprise as he bent and simply lifted her off her feet to lower her down into the launch tied up by the jetty. She winced at his words though, wishing he wouldn't remind her of her brother's lowest moment and worst mistake. 'You still haven't said where we're going… You said I didn't need to get changed and now I'm wearing a wedding dress in a boat.'

'To board a much larger vessel,' Tor sliced in, indicating the huge yacht anchored out in the bay and silhouetted against the starry night sky.

'You own a yacht?'

'No. It belongs to a family friend and his wedding present is the use of it. If you like cruising we can always buy one,' he told her as the launch bounced over the sea at speed, driven by the crew member in charge of the wheel.

Pixie studied the yacht with wide eyes, struggling to accept that she was now living in a world where her bridegroom could talk carelessly about purchasing such an enormous luxury. 'Why haven't you bought one already?'

'To date, I haven't taken much time away from work and a yacht would have been a superfluous purchase for a workaholic. But that has to change with you and Alfie in my life now,' Tor traded calmly.

She wanted to ask him if he had been an absentee husband and father during his first marriage, but on their own wedding day it felt as if that would be tacky and untimely. He had made her wary of impulsive speech as well when he had reacted badly to a tactless question earlier that day. For that reason, she made no comment and bore up beautifully to being hoisted on board the enormous yacht in her fancy gown and greeted by the captain and a glass of champagne before being guided up to the top deck and a bedroom that took her breath away.

'I'm afraid that we now need to have a serious discussion about your brother,' Tor murmured levelly then, utterly taking her aback with that announcement.

Bright blue eyes widening in bewilderment, Pixie slowly swivelled, silk momentarily tightening across her slender, shapely figure to draw his magnetic gaze. 'What on earth are you talking about?'

'Today of all days, I don't want you to be upset,' Tor informed her smoothly. 'But I believe that Jordan was the source of a rather sleazy story about our first night together and Alfie that appeared in a British newspaper this morning—'

A fury unlike anything Pixie had ever felt, or indeed had even guessed she *could* feel, burned up her backbone like a licking flame and she went rigid with the force of it. 'Is that so?' she almost whispered.

'Who else could it be but Jordan?' Tor derided. 'He'll do anything for money. He has no decency, no backbone.'

'Shut up!' Pixie practically spat at him in her outrage at that denunciation.

His brows knotted, a look of incredulity in his smouldering golden eyes, such incivility not having featured very often in his experience. '*Diavolos*, Pixie. There is no reason for you to treat this as though it is some kind of personal attack on *you*. It is not intended as such.'

And Tor stood there, smokingly handsome, thrillingly sexy and towering over her. He was utterly sure of his ground in a fashion that she supposed came entirely naturally to him and yet she wanted to kill him in that instant, smite him down with heavenly lightning for blaming her poor brother for the tabloid article as well. As though Jordan had not already sinned enough and *paid* the price for his mistakes! He had lost her respect and the only home he had ever known, and his self-esteem was at basement level. And yes, he had deserved that punishment, but right now he was trying very hard to fix himself and pick himself up again, only he hadn't yet mustered sufficient strength to make more than a couple of tottering steps back towards normality. At present, in her view, Jordan was more to be pitied than condemned.

'Yes, shut up and stop talking down to me in that patronising way!' Pixie let fly at Tor angrily again. 'I gather you haven't actually *seen* that article. Well, before you hang, draw and quarter my brother for the story, acquaint yourself with the article and the facts first.'

'Have you seen it? I assumed you didn't know about it,' Tor confided in disconcertion. 'I didn't mention it because I didn't want to destroy the day.'

'So, you just destroyed it now instead by assuming that Jordan is to blame when in fact it is *your own choices* that brought the humiliation of that article down on the two of us!' Pixie flung back at him in a furious counter-attack.

'How could it be anything to do with *my* choices?' Tor shot back at her icily, his own temper rising because he had not been prepared for either her attitude or the argument that had erupted. Unsurprisingly, he would never have chosen to mention the article on their wedding night had he foreseen her response.

'Look it up online and find out, as I had to,' Pixie urged him curtly.

Tor did nothing so basic. He shot an order to one of his personal assistants to send him an exact copy of the item, still outraged that *his* assumptions, *his* conclusions, were being questioned.

First, a photo of a woman he had never seen in his life before arrived on his screen, and he turned it towards Pixie and breathed, 'Who is she?'

'Saffron Wells—an actress. The beauty who brought you back to the house that night. You allowed her to pick you up and bring you back there and I suspect that she saw you leaving the room I was using the next morning.'

'I don't know what you're talking about and you know it!' Tor thundered at her, while grudgingly recalling that vague memory of someone coming down the stairs in that house that morning. Disorientated and in a bad mood, he hadn't even turned round to see who it was. 'Because you flatly *refused* to tell me everything about that night!'

Pixie was in no mood to compromise when she was still so angry with him. On a level she didn't want to examine, some of her anger related to the weirdest current of possessiveness inside her. It still annoyed her that he had allowed Saffron to pick him up, even if he hadn't done anything with the other woman, and even though she knew she would never have met him otherwise, that annoyance went surprisingly deep.

'Saffron brought you back to the house in the first place. You apparently believed you were accompanying her to a party, but she thought she was bringing you home for the night. You rejected her because supposedly you weren't in the mood and she stormed off… At least that's what *you* told me happened. But for all I know,' Pixie breathed with withering bite, 'you slept with her too before I came into the kitchen, where you were waiting for a taxi!'

Tor swore in vicious Greek at being slapped in the face with that character assassination. 'I may have been drunk, I may have slept with you that night, but I'm no playboy and you know it.'

'According to your online images, you've been around…*a lot*,' Pixie emphasised, unimpressed. 'However, I'd say it's unlikely anything happened between you because I think you offended her and that's one good reason why she sold that story. Her being passed over for someone as ordinary as me would have been the last straw. The other reason is that, being a media person, she lapped up the opportunity to get her picture into a newspaper.'

Tor was frowning now. 'But if she was some

random woman in that house, how could she possibly have known about you getting pregnant and all the rest of it when you left the property only a couple of days later?'

'There were other connections involved. I was using Steph's room that night. Steph was one of the other tenants and I worked with her sister. I had ongoing contact with Steph because of my cat, Coco. Steph only finally gave Coco to me when I was pregnant,' Pixie recited wearily, the fury draining from her without warning. 'Someone somewhere talked and connected the dots and that's how the story about us got out. It had nothing at all to do with my brother, who knew less than you did about what happened that night until very recently.'

His lean dark features hard and forbidding, Tor jerked his chin in acknowledgement of that likelihood. He was angry because he had got it badly wrong again with his bride. He was angry because he had been so *sure* of his facts when a thieving, dishonest, greedy character, such as he regarded Jordan to be, had been in the mix and available to blame. But he was still stunned by the level of her loyalty to her brother, her childhood memories of the other man evidently sufficient to restore some measure of her faith and affection for him.

Her attitude made him think of his own response to Sevastiano, the older brother he had only met when they were both adults. Tor had found it an un-

nerving experience to go from being the eldest son
in the family to the discovery that his father's eldest
child had actually been born to another woman before his marriage to Tor's mother. If he was honest,
he had never really given Sevastiano a fair crack of
the whip and learning that Katerina had been unfaithful to him *with* Sev had been the last nail in
the coffin. No semblance of sibling affection had
ever developed.

Shaking off that momentary attack of self-
examination, Tor straightened his broad shoulders.
'I owe you an apology,' he breathed between gritted
teeth. 'But make some allowances for the difference between our natures. When it comes to your
brother, I'm less forgiving of his wrongs towards
you and my son and much more about punishment,
while you're overflowing with compassion and a
desperate desire to rehabilitate him. But please accept that *my* strongest motivation is to protect you
from Jordan and ensure that he cannot take advantage of you or hurt you again.'

Pixie nodded jerkily, tears stinging the backs of
her eyes because this was not how she had imagined her wedding night would turn out, with them at
loggerheads, angry words having been exchanged
and now all the subsequent discomfiture of the aftermath. 'Apology accepted,' she said stiffly, crossing the room to explore through a door and discover
to her relief that it led into a bathroom where she

could excusably escape for long enough to regroup. 'I'm going to treat myself to a bath…if you don't mind?'

'Of course not,' Tor murmured tautly, wondering how to dig himself back out of the hole he had dug for himself and coming up blank from lack of practice in that field.

'I need your help to undo the hooks on this dress,' Pixie admitted even more stiffly. 'I don't want to damage it. Being a sentimental sort, I want to keep it.'

Tor breathed in deep and slow, questioning how the hell he had once again screwed up with her when such errors and misunderstandings had never occurred with any other woman. He was all over the place inside his head: he could *feel* it and it unnerved him more than a little to appreciate that, with her, he lost his focus, his self-discipline and his logical cool. She had shouted at him and he had not even known she was *capable* of shouting because in so many ways she was his exact opposite, being gentle and caring and softer in every way. Softer but *not* weak, he grasped, grateful for that distinction, because her weasel-like brother's weakness had turned his stomach.

'I like that,' he admitted honestly. 'You're not thinking of me having a successor.'

Pixie twisted her head round to survey him in shock. 'You thought that might have been likely?'

'It's not uncommon in my world for a woman to use her first marriage as a stepping stone to better.'

'You're Alfie's father. I couldn't get better,' she insisted awkwardly.

'Even though I messed up?'

'Everyone does that occasionally,' Pixie pointed out, shooting him a sideways smile as he embarked on the hooks on her silk gown. 'Sooner or later I'm going to do it too…nothing surer.'

'You always say the right forgiving thing, don't you?'

'Well, it's better than being all bitter and cynical and always expecting the worst from people, which seems to be your MO…*not* trying to start another argument!' she added in haste.

'I see the world through a different lens. I'm not bitter,' Tor asserted.

Pixie would have begged to differ on that score, but she compressed her lips and said nothing at all. Of course, Tor was bitter that his first love had let him down so badly, but if he was determined not to recognise the fact. that was *his* business, not hers. It wasn't his fault that he didn't know enough about his own emotions to label them, was it? Because she had decided that *that* was what she was dealing with: a guy utterly unable to recognise his own feelings for what they were, blind as a bat to his own emotional promptings. He had concentrated on the guilt he'd experienced at his wife and daughter's deaths, beat himself up for his mistakes rather than on the huge betrayal that had preceded and powered that tragic loss.

Tor's usually nimble fingers began to get inexplicably clumsy as he unhooked the back of Pixie's dress. Pale pearly shoulder blades, narrow and delicate, were revealed, and as the hooks worked down, something frilly and lacy and absolutely Tor's favourite sort of lingerie began to appear and he snatched in a startled breath, wondering why it felt vaguely indecent to find his bride quite so sexually potent. It was a tiny corset, as tiny as she was as long as she didn't turn round and show off the front view, which he imagined would be spectacular. He reminded himself that she was heading for a bath and that the last thing she needed now was to be mauled by a sexually voracious bridegroom, who had already infuriated her. He spread the corners of the gown back and succumbed involuntarily to temptation, pressing his lips softly against an inch of pale porcelain skin.

'Tor…?' Pixie prompted, but only after a helpless little quiver as that unsought kiss on her skin travelled through her.

'Working on the hooks,' Tor ground out thickly, watching the corset hooks appear, the pulse at his groin speeding from interested to crazed because he was realising just what he had wrecked. The fancy lingerie had been for *his* benefit because he

had made that remark about how much he liked
such adornments.

'I find you incredibly tempting,' he breathed
with a ragged undertone as he traced the line of
her shoulder to her nape with the tip of his tongue
and lingered there, drinking in the fruit scent of her
skin, some kind of peachy scent that absolutely did
it for him. 'I'm sorry.'

Pixie wasn't really speaking to Tor, not in a
childish way but in a grown-up-quiet way. She had
been en route to a bath and a serious rethink about
where she stood with him, but nobody had ever
told her that she was incredibly tempting before.
No man's hand had ever trembled before against
her shoulder and that she could have the power to
affect Tor to that extent was a dream come true for
her. Slowly, Pixie turned round and let the silk dress
drop down her arms to her wrists and fall, so that
the whole thing dropped round her ankles and he
was gratifyingly entranced. It was written all over
him, brilliant dark golden eyes locked to her like
magnets, and she liked that, really, *really* liked that.

'Kiss me,' she said abruptly, not thinking about
it, *refusing* to think about it, just acting on natural instinct.

'That's where we started out before.'

'Nothing wrong with a repeat,' Pixie told him
squarely. 'But you're far too tall to kiss standing

upright, so I think we should move…er…lie down, whatever.'

'You were going for a bath.' Tor husked the reminder reluctantly.

'A lady can change her mind,' Pixie told him, drowning in the dark golden smouldering depths of his black-fringed eyes, revelling in the truth that the gorgeous guy was actually *her* gorgeous guy and not someone else's.

'Did I say sorry *that* well?' Tor asked, sucking in a quick shallow breath, quite unbelievably enthralled by her change of heart and shocked by himself.

'I'm softer than you but selfish too,' Pixie whispered shakily. 'I want you. I probably want you more than I ever wanted anything in my life.'

And that was the green light that Tor needed to snatch her up out of her fallen gown and carry her over to the bed, where he laid her out to admire her in all the glory of the white corset, panties and white stockings she had worn for his benefit. He couldn't take his eyes off her tiny figure lying on display, the full mounds of her breasts cupped in lace for his delectation, the tight white vee of silk between her thighs, the slender graceful line of her thighs. He was enchanted by that view. Dimly, he registered that sex had, evidently, been rather boring before he met Pixie, something only his strong libido had driven him to do on a regular basis, and that was a fine distinction he had not recognised before. *She* made him burn with lust, *she* added another entire dimension to his concept of sexual desire.

Without warning, Pixie scrambled up and off the bed and began to help him out of his jacket. 'You've got too much on,' she mumbled, half under her breath, belatedly embarrassed by her own boldness.

Tor smiled, shed the tie, the jacket, peeled off his shirt and toed off his shoes. He was getting rid of the socks and unzipping his trousers when he saw her seated at the foot of the wide divan watching him as though he were a film. 'What?' he queried with a raised brow.

'You didn't undress the first time,' Pixie admitted starkly.

And in that single admission, Tor knew how badly he had got it wrong the night his son had been conceived and he almost grimaced. 'Precautions?'

Pixie winced and reddened. 'No, neither of us thought of that, so that wasn't entirely your fault. I was foolish too.'

His black brows drew together. 'I was fully clothed when I woke up the next day, which is why I had no idea I had been intimate with anyone,' he breathed in a driven undertone, because nothing that he was discovering was raising his opinion of himself when he was under the influence of alcohol

and he knew it would be a cold day in hell before
he got in that condition again.

Pixie dropped her curly head with a wincing motion of her slight shoulders. 'I…er…tidied you up. I
was… I was embarrassed… If I'm honest, I didn't
want you to know or remember me. I felt I had let
myself down and taken advantage of you.'

'Of…*me*?' Tor cited in disbelief.

'Well, you'd been quite clear about not wanting
to be with anyone after you had rejected Saffron,'
she reminded him ruefully. 'I should've heeded that
and drawn back.'

Tor set his teeth together. 'We both got carried
away and I know why. You turn me on fast and hard
and neither of us was able to call a halt.'

Pixie nodded in a rush, seeing that he had
grasped what had happened, the sheer explosion of
hunger that had seized her. But while they had been
talking, Tor had also been getting naked and her
mind was wandering because she was very much
enjoying the view. Stripped down to black boxers,
he had the build of a Greek god garbed in living
flesh instead of marble and the lean, powerful lines
of muscle etching his chest and abdomen made her
mouth run dry. He was amazingly perfect and beautiful. In Eloise's parlance, it was a case of the super
tanker and the tugboat comparison again. What on
earth had he *ever* seen in her ordinary self? Or was
that kind of physical attraction simply unquantifi-

able and impossible to explain? she wondered. The pull between them that night had been so strong, so irresistible and already she could feel the same thing happening to her again, her body warming and quickening down deep inside and her heartbeat speeding up.

'Tonight will be different from that first night,' Tor swore with an edge of raw anticipation and masculine resolve that sent butterflies cascading through her stomach while a hot, tight feeling clenched her pelvis.

CHAPTER NINE

'It wasn't a bad experience…er…you and me,' Pixie reassured him with hot cheeks. 'Physically it worked for me.'

'I can do better than that,' Tor husked, staring down at her, at the high plump mounds peaking from the lace edge of the corset. 'I love this lingerie, *hara mou*.'

'You're acting like it's something special to you…me wearing this stuff,' Pixie muttered tensely. 'When we both know it's *not* special because you've had many women in your life and a great deal of experience.'

'After Katerina I never stayed with anyone for more than a few days, so I was never around long enough for anyone to make the effort to dress up for me,' he countered bluntly as he gazed down at her with heavily lashed, half-hooded, dark brooding eyes. 'We're married now. This is a whole different relationship.'

Yes, very different from the one he must once
have had with the woman he loved, Pixie's brain
sniped, and she stifled that thought, knowing that
such thoughts, such pointless, tasteless comparisons, would drive her mad if she let them in. Katerina was his past and *she* was his present and she
had to be sensible and view their marriage in that
positive light, not give way to envy. *Envy?* That was
what she was discovering inside herself, a sense
of envy relating to his late wife, who had had it
all with him and simply thrown it away. Why *was*
she envious? Why was she feeling more than she
should about an old relationship that was none of
her business?

But that knotty question fled her mind as Tor
brought her down on the bed and crushed her mouth
under his. If there was one thing she had learned the
first time Tor kissed her, it was that Tor knew how
to kiss, indeed, Tor knew so well how to kiss that
he made her head spin and sent a ripple of craving
shooting through her with every dancing plunge of
his tongue. Her fingers laced into the thick silk of
his hair and held him to her, smoothing down over
his wide, strong shoulders, exploring over the satin
skin of his back because that first night she hadn't
been able to touch him while he was still clothed.

Tor came up on an elbow, a long forefinger skim-
ming back an edge of lace to bare a rounded breast
crowned by a straining pink nipple. 'You excite the

hell out of me,' he admitted gruffly, hungrily closing a mouth to that tempting peak, using the tip of his tongue, the tug of his teeth and his warm sensual mouth to pleasure her.

The motion of his mouth on her breasts tightened her, as if there were a chain leading to the hot, liquid centre of her body, and her hips shifted upwards, all of her awash with more craving. He sat her up with easy confidence and began to unhook the corset. Her cheeks flushed and she looked away from him, wanting so much to own that confidence of his. It had been dim that first night, never mind his lack of awareness: he had not been looking for flaws.

'What's wrong?' he asked her, disconcerting her by noticing her anxiety.

'It was sort of darkish that night and now I feel like I'm under floodlights.' With one hand she made an awkward motion towards the fancy lights above, the mirrors on the units adding their myriad reflections to the brightness.

Tor shifted up and hit a switch above the bed and the illumination dimmed. 'Better?'

'It's really stupid being shy when we've already got a kid,' Pixie muttered guiltily, wishing she could get a grip on her self-consciousness before it wrecked the atmosphere.

'No, it's not.' Tor tugged her back down to him, moulding his big hands to her full breasts. 'But you do stress a lot, don't you?'

'Yes,' she admitted ruefully.

'So, it's up to me to ensure you have more to think about, *latria mou...*' Tor skated a fingertip across the taut triangle of her panties and she gasped, the pulse of arousal between her slender thighs kicking on to an intense high.

In that moment everything else melted away along with her insecurities. Suddenly, she was twisting round to find that wicked mouth of his, so sensually full and yet hard and soft at the same time, that so enthralled her. He was peeling off her panties and she quivered at the prospect of him touching her again, for the merest instant mortified by her own eagerness, but then she was already maddeningly conscious of the swollen, slick readiness of her own body.

Even the lightest brush of his fingertips aroused her, and she was knocked off balance when he slid down the bed and began to use his mouth on that most tender area. Of course, she knew about that, knew the specifics of everything sexual, but she hadn't ever imagined that anything could feel as good as what he made her feel then. Every nerve ending in her body seemed to be centred there and before very long she was quivering with little reflexive tremors running through her and breathless little sounds she couldn't silence falling from her parted lips as her head thrashed back and forth on the pillow.

As the pressure in her pelvis rose and tightened, her hips began to writhe to a spontaneous rhythm and the great gathering whoosh of sensation surged and she cried out and then lay there, discovering her fingers were knotted in his hair and slowly withdrawing them, a great lassitude sweeping her.

'No, you don't get to sleep now, *moraki mou*,' Tor told her with a slashing grin that banished every shred of dark, forbidding tension from his lean, darkly handsome features. He kissed her with devouring hunger as he stretched up over her with the lean, powerful, predatory grace of a stalking panther. She tasted herself on his lips and still moaned beneath that sensual assault as he hooked up her knees and settled her back, pushing his hot, sleek shaft against the still-tingling entrance to her body and plunging in hard enough to make her gasp in delight.

He angled down his hips and sank so deep into her that she didn't know where he began and she ended and that was only the beginning, the wildly arousing beginning while she was still in control. But the excitement of his fluid, driving thrusts into her sensitised body smashed her control, smashed it and broke it into tiny pieces until she was rising against him with her heart pounding and her body arching, craving his every move. She could barely breathe, she could certainly not speak, but had she had her voice she would only have urged him *not to stop.* The burning rise to orgasm began all over again, forcing her higher and higher, stimulated almost beyond bearing and seething with a physical sensual energy she had not known she possessed. And then at the zenith of sensation she shattered, electrified by the blazing excitement that convulsed her every limb, and she was utterly captivated by the drenching slow, sweet pleasure that flooded her in the aftermath.

Tor froze as Pixie cuddled into him, her little hand spreading across the centre of his damp heaving chest, and for an instant he almost lost control and pushed her away from him in a knee-jerk reaction. For five years, he had been pushing women away the instant they tried to be affectionate because, rather than pleasing him, it chilled him. It had always reminded him of Katerina's superficial affection, which had, in the end, proved to be so false, not only towards him, but towards her daughter as well, he acknowledged grimly. But he would not make vile comparisons that Pixie did not deserve, and he would make a really big effort to pretend that this was his first marriage *before* he learned to question almost everything a woman said and did.

That sounded bitter, he conceded in surprise as he extended an arm round Pixie's slight, pliant body and pulled her close. But he wasn't bitter—*was he? Thee mou*, his bride was as good as a witch when it came to slotting odd ideas into his mind! Only, she didn't need a book to cast a spell, only her body, her response, her warmth, all of which she offered so freely. If he wasn't very careful he would hurt her again, because she was much more fragile than the women he was accustomed to dealing with and he wasn't of a sensitive persuasion.

'Is it always that amazing?' Pixie whispered.

'No, it's not,' Tor answered truthfully, and he was almost but not quite tempted to tell her that it had never been that good for him before, but she didn't need to know that, did she? Theirs was a marriage of convenience and practicality and that was *all* he wanted it to be. He didn't want the legendary highs or the fabled lows, he would be content with his son and a marriage on an even keel.

Pixie felt blissfully relaxed, relieved that the silly newspaper story had been dealt with and set aside without causing more trouble. Being in a relationship, being one half of a whole, was very new to her and she was beginning to see that there were no hard and fast rules and that she had to learn to compromise and smooth over the rough spots where she could. Even now, though, she was aware that even if Tor didn't see it, he was still damaged by what Katerina had done to him.

Pixie had felt him freeze when she'd snuggled up to him and she had held her breath, waiting to see what he would do, and she had only relaxed when he'd pulled her the rest of the way into his arms. But that didn't mean that she wasn't aware that she had married a wary, bitter, suspicious man with a tendency to expect everything to blow up in his face when he least expected it. Hopefully, time and experience would teach him differently when it came to having her and Alfie as a family. Should how he felt matter to her as much as it did? Well, she knew what her problem was: she was halfway to falling madly in love with Tor, possibly even further than halfway, she conceded ruefully.

Almost a month later, Pixie watched Tor climb, still dripping, from the pool, after the acrobatics he had performed there to entertain Alfie, and cross the main deck to speak to the yacht captain, a bearded man currently sporting an apologetic smile.

While they were chatting she lifted Alfie, who was already half-asleep, and moved down to the cabin where her son was sleeping to change him and put him in his crib for a nap. Their nanny, Isla, was probably sunbathing on the top deck because Pixie and Tor usually kept Alfie with them in the mornings. She went for a shower and was towelling herself dry when Tor reappeared in the doorway.

'We have an unscheduled stop to make this evening to take on supplies. While the crew are dealing with stocking up, we'll be enjoying a sheltered cove and dining in a restaurant which the captain assures me is a hidden gem,' he related lazily as he peeled off his shorts.

Heat mushroomed in her pelvis as she watched and dimly wondered if she would ever become accustomed to Tor's utterly stunning masculine beauty. His gleaming bronzed gaze struck hers and she stilled, her heartbeat quickening, her breath catching in her throat. *'Se thelo,'* he breathed, thick and low.

I want you—one little Greek phrase she had become hugely familiar with over the past four weeks.

Hunger lightening his eyes to gold, he reached for her, disposing of the towel with an aggressive jerk to release her small body from its folds and hauling her up against his hard, hot length.

'I *always* want you,' he breathed with a slight frown, as if he couldn't quite work out why that should be so. 'You're turning me into a sex addict.'

Pixie flushed, knowing that she matched him there. She couldn't keep her hands off him, couldn't back off from the allure of that raw masculine magnetism he emanated if her life depended on it. It flared in her every time she looked at him, every time he reached for her, like a flame that had only been fed into a blaze by constant proximity. A month was a long time for a couple to be alone together, she acknowledged, just a little sad that they would be returning to London the following day. It had been a wonderful holiday though, *her*

honeymoon, something she had not been quite sure
it was when they'd first set sail on their wedding
night. But they had both needed that time and space
to get to know each other on a deeper level and it
had worked. Tor had probably planned it that way,
she conceded, having finally come to understand
that Tor planned most things. It was just the way
he operated. Only with sex was Tor spontaneous
or impulsive.

'What's wrong?' Tor husked as he backed her
into the cabin again, all hungry predatory resolve
and indescribably sexy in the role.

'Absolutely nothing,' she told him truthfully, because she reckoned that she would have to be a very
demanding person to want more from him than she
already had, and she refused to allow herself to feel
discontented.

He spread her out on the bed and she tingled all
over, her skin prickling with high-voltage awareness
and anticipation as he feathered his sensual mouth
over her protuberant nipples, making her moan. He
stroked a provocative fingertip between her legs,
where she was already swollen and damp, and a
fierce smile of satisfaction slanted his lean, darkly
handsome features. Without any further preamble,
he thrust into her hard and fast and a shot of dynamite pleasure ravaged her pliant body. His compelling rhythm sent her to a stormy height of need
faster than she would have believed. It was good,

it was *so* good she climaxed crying out his name…
and something else. 'I love you!' she gasped, just
seconds before her brain could kick in again and
make her swallow those words.

And Tor said…*nothing*. Pixie told herself that
possibly he hadn't heard or that he was just politely
ignoring that accidental word spillage of hers and
that that was better than forcing her to discuss the
issue. For Tor would see that declaration as an issue,
not a benefit, not a compliment, not something he
should treasure and be grateful for. In turmoil, she
turned away from him, her face literally burning
with mortification and a sense of humiliation. Why?
Why had she had to let those words escape?

Maybe it was pathetic to be so happy with a guy
who didn't love her when deep down inside her
there was still this dangerous nagging need to have
more from him and, of course, it bothered her. After
all, love couldn't be turned on like a magic tap by
anyone but perhaps, over time, Tor would come to
care for her more, she had recently soothed herself.
Life wasn't a fairy tale, Eloise had warned her, but,
in truth, Pixie couldn't help still yearning for the
fairy tale.

Yet at the same time, honesty lay at the very
heart of her nature and she had wanted to share her
feelings with Tor, give him that warmth and validation. After all, she knew for a fact that life could
change in a moment with an accident, an illness,

some other terrible event, and she needed to live in the moment. Secrets weren't her style.

It was true though that there were still little black holes in their relationship where she didn't dare travel. He never ever talked about Katerina or Sofia, not even accidentally. It was as if he had locked that all up in some underground box on the night of the crash when he'd lost his wife and child and, sadly, only an excess of alcohol had unleashed his devastating emotional confessions the evening he and Pixie had first met. The rest of the time? Tor might as well have been a single man rather than a widower when she'd married him.

Yet Tor had asked her so much about her parents and her childhood memories, had freely satisfied his own curiosity and it had brought them closer, of course it had. Why couldn't he do the same for her when it came to his first marriage? His silence was a barrier that disturbed her. Why was he still holding back? It was because of her honesty that Tor now understood a great deal better why she was so attached to her half-brother, the boy who had stood up for her in the playground when other children had teased her about her diminutive size, the adult male who had comforted her after the death of their father and her mother by promising that he would always be there for her.

'Need a shower,' she muttered, pulling free of the arms anchored round her and heading for the bathroom as though her life depended on it because his silence hurt her. Was it possible that he was still in love with his dead wife? Or was she being fanciful?

Tor rolled over and punched a pillow, perfect white teeth clenching now that Pixie was out of view. For a split second he was furious with her for putting him in that position. Just because he wasn't prepared to lie, wasn't prepared to pretend! Those three words were so easy to say, had routinely featured between him and Katerina and they had been absolutely meaningless and empty on her side.

But was it fair to punish Pixie for Katerina's lies and pretences?

He froze as that possibility penetrated his brain for the very first time. He wasn't punishing anybody, he roared defensively inside himself. He was simply insisting on a higher standard of honesty in their marriage, which meant that there would be a smaller chance of misunderstandings occurring between them. They needed a lot of things in a successful marriage, but love wasn't a necessity, not as respect and loyalty and caring were, he reasoned in exasperation. Pixie was just young and rather naïve and had yet to grasp such fine distinctions. And it wasn't as though believing that she loved him was likely to do her any harm, he rationalised, denying the warmth spreading through his chest and the smile tugging at the corners of his mouth.

* * *

That evening Pixie dressed to go ashore for dinner in a glorious white sundress that flattered her new tan, her blond curls tumbling round her shoulders in abundance. Her wardrobe had expanded over the month because Tor had taken her to more than one exclusive shopping outlet where he had insisted on buying her stuff. Jewellery such as she had never expected to own sparkled in the diamonds at her ears and throat, the slender gold watch on her wrist, the glittering rings on her fingers. On the outside she looked like a rich woman; on the inside, though, she still felt like an imposter, she acknowledged unhappily. She had won Katerina's place only by the other woman's death and an accidental conception. She was basically just Katerina's imperfect replacement and even Alfie was only a replacement for the little girl who had died.

The launch delivered her and Tor to a beach, where he insisted on carrying her across to the steps that wound up the cliff to where the restaurant sat. Pixie examined her feelings for him as he set her carefully down on the steps, so attentive, so honourable, so everything but *not* loving. How could she condemn him for that lack? she scolded herself sharply, annoyed that she was letting her own humiliation linger and twist her up to the detriment of their marriage. That was foolish, short-sighted, and in the light of that reflection she linked her arms round his neck before he could straighten and stretched up to kiss him. He didn't have to love her because she loved him; they could get by fine as they were.

Relief coursed through Tor, who had remained insanely conscious of how quiet and muted Pixie had become throughout the day. He didn't know when he had become so attuned to her moods, but he noticed the instant the sparkle died in her eyes and she withdrew from him. It had disconcerted him to appreciate how much she could put him on edge. He smiled at her as he urged her up the steps, careful to stay behind her in case she stumbled in her high heels. They took seats out on the terrace with its panoramic view of the sea and had only received their menus when Tor swore softly in surprise under his breath.

An older couple had walked out onto the terrace.

'My godparents,' he breathed. 'Basil and Dimitra... *not* a happy coincidence.'

'I think I dimly remember them from the wedding... but we didn't actually speak,' Pixie whispered. 'Don't you like them?'

'It's not that,' Tor parried with a frown before he stood up to greet the other couple.

Pixie rose as well, walking into a hail of Greek being exchanged and smiling valiantly. Dimitra introduced herself in easy English, explaining that she had grown up in London before moving to Greece in her teens, where she had gone to school with Tor's mother, Pandora. Their meeting was not quite the coincidence Tor had stated, Pixie thought once she learned that the other couple owned a holiday home nearby. Tor insisted that the couple join them for their meal, and it passed pleasantly with talk of their cruise round the Greek islands until Tor became increasingly involved in talking business with his godfather. By the coffee stage, the men had shifted to the outside bar across the terrace and the two women were alone.

'I feel guilty that we've intruded on your last night away.' Dimitra sighed.

'I'm really surprised that I didn't get talking to you at the wedding when you're so close to Hallas and Pandora,' Pixie confided, wondering how that oversight had come about.

'I suppose because we felt it would've been inappropriate to put ourselves forward too much. I wasn't even sure about us accepting the invitation to your wedding,' Dimitra admitted and, seeing Pixie's frowning, puzzled look, added, 'You don't know, do you? Tor's first wife was *our* daughter...'

'Oh...' Pixie whispered, bereft of breath by that revelation but equally quickly grasping the difficulties of that situation. 'But you're all still good friends, aren't you?'

'Of course, although it's a shame that Tor chose to conceal the truth about their marriage,' Dimitra

shared in a troubled undertone. 'After what he'd
endured, we've never wanted to tackle that subject
with him directly, but we're straight-talking people
and it would've been easier for us had he just admitted that our daughter was having an affair and
that Sofia was not his. At first I was grateful for
that silence but with such close friends I would've
preferred the truth rather than feeling forced to live
a lie.'

Pixie settled startled eyes on the other woman,
swiftly suppressing the shock of learning that Sofia
had *not*, after all, been Tor's child. 'I don't think Tor
realises that *you* know.'

'We knew. We tried hard to stop it, but we got
nowhere. Katerina was obsessed with Devon.'

Pixie's brow furrowed. 'Devon?' she queried.

'Sevastiano's half-brother, Devon. Katerina
called him Dev. Ironically, they met at a prewedding
party Hallas and Pandora threw for Tor and my
daughter. Devon was already married with two
young children,' Dimitra revealed heavily. 'But
once Tor and Katerina moved to London, where
Devon lived, the fact that they were both married
didn't influence either of them and we didn't know
it was happening until two years after the marriage
when we caught them together. It was on that hor-
rible day that my daughter admitted that she was
pregnant with Devon's child. I won't go into our
feelings, but you can imagine how treacherous I

felt when Pandora wept over the passing of a child who was not of their blood. But it was not *our* secret to tell.'

And Tor hadn't revealed that final secret even when he *could* have told it that first night they met, Pixie reflected painfully. Even more revealing was his silence on that score, a silence so complete, so unyielding over the entire sordid business that he had been erroneously blaming his brother, Sevastiano, for being his late wife's lover when in fact it had not been him. How on earth had he contrived to get *that* wrong? Yet it served Tor right, a part of Pixie declared *without* sympathy. He had been far too busy hugging his damaged ego and his secrets, and Tor and his family had remained in dangerous ignorance long after the event. And that was very unhealthy, wasn't it?

A welter of differing thoughts and deductions assailed Pixie on the launch that wafted them back to the yacht. What she had learned from Dimitra had put her in an awkward position. She had to tell Tor not only that his former in-laws were already fully acquainted with their late daughter's peccadilloes, but also that he had misjudged his brother, Sevastiano, who had not been Katerina's lover. How could she keep quiet about such matters? They were too important to ignore yet too personal for her to want to tackle them...aside of that revelation about

Sofia, who had not been Tor's daughter, as he had led her to believe.

But did Tor even know that Sofia had not been his child? It was perfectly possible that he didn't know, Pixie reasoned uneasily. On the other hand, if he *did* know, Pixie believed that Tor should have told *her*—because such an issue *did* matter to the mother of the baby she had assumed to be his second child.

However, if Dimitra was to be believed, Alfie was Tor's firstborn, and if he had known that all along and kept quiet about it, deliberately misleading Pixie in relation to her son's status, she *did* have a bone to pick with him. Just at that moment Pixie felt very tired of following in Katerina's footsteps and suspecting that her beloved Alfie was a mere replacement for Tor's lost daughter. All of a sudden that felt like a burning issue for her. But at the same time she was consumed by the awareness of what Tor must have suffered when he'd realised that the child he loved was not his child, and she felt quite sick at the prospect of having to broach that topic with him.

'You're very quiet. Did Dimitra say something that upset you? I didn't intend to leave you alone. Basil had a tricky financial problem he wanted my advice on and I lost track of time.'

'No, nothing she said upset me,' Pixie lied, because she didn't want him misinterpreting her

meaning. 'Although I could've done with you just
biting the bullet and telling me that your godparents
are your former in-laws. It's not such a big deal.'

'It feels awkward now that I've remarried,' Tor
countered a little stiffly. 'Especially with all that
happened five years ago. I've known them all my
life but I'm aware that they feel uncomfortable as
well. It's unfortunate. They're a lovely couple.'

'Yes. I liked them,' Pixie confided, on surer
ground.

'It's a mystery to me why their daughters turned
out as they did. Maybe they spoilt them, never told
them no... I don't know. I feel like I should know,
though, when I grew up with them running around
my home, but you have a different viewpoint as a
child.'

'I didn't know there was another daughter.'

'Angelina. Didn't you meet her at the wedding?'
Tor asked casually.

'Oh, yes, I met her, but I didn't realise the connection.' Pixie understood Angelina's bad attitude then,
or thought she did: a sister being confronted by her
dead sibling's replacement bride and child. The brunette had been unpleasant but her identity granted
her some excuse for her behaviour, in Pixie's opinion.

Her mind moved on as she mulled over Tor's
remark about it being a mystery how the Raptis
daughters had turned out as they had. That was the
closest he had ever come to criticising Katerina and

it surprised her, for she had assumed that he still viewed his first wife as some kind of misunderstood martyr.

'We have to talk when we get back,' she breathed softly as Tor settled her down in a seat on the launch, having carried her across the beach to save her from the task of removing her shoes.

'About what?'

'Stuff,' she framed flatly.

His ebony brows pleated, bronzed eyes narrowing with a dark glitter in the moonlight, and she thought how gorgeous his sculpted bone structure was and of the marvel that she was actually married to such a man. All that electrifying sexiness and caring and she was still finding fault? Was she crazy?

CHAPTER TEN

TOR HAD SPENT much of the evening lazily watching his wife across the depth of the terrace, drinking in her natural animation, the shine of her naturally blond curls below the lights, the deep ocean blueness of her eyes and the amazing curves hinted at even below that perfectly modest sundress. Where she was concerned, he was like a junkie in constant need of a fix, he reflected grimly, because that lack of control, that burning hunger that continually seethed in him, bothered him. Something about Pixie revved his libido to absurd heights and, always a fan of everything in moderation, he had already tried and failed abysmally to switch off that reaction or at the very least turn it down to a more acceptable level.

And what did she want to talk about? He could think of nothing amiss and that put him on edge as well because he didn't like surprises. In his past experience a surprise had rarely led to anything good and yet Pixie regularly surprised him in the most positive of ways. She was a terrific mother to his son, protective without overdoing it, loving and caring and willing to share Alfie. She was unsophisticated, naïve, utterly ignorant of the exclusive world he inhabited and yet she moved through that same world with disconcerting grace and assurance, relying on ordinary courtesy to smooth her path. When he least expected it, she impressed him, and she had done it over and over again.

On board the yacht again, Pixie walked ahead of him up to their master cabin, where most of their luggage had already been packed ready for their departure back to London. First thing in the morning they were being picked up by a helicopter, which would deliver them straight to the airport.

'We can talk when we get back to London,' she suggested rather abruptly, apprehensive about the confrontation that she knew awaited her. It cut her to the heart that Tor had *not* chosen to confide in her about the truth that he had not been Sofia's father. That revelation on top of Katerina's infidelity must have devastated him. Yet Pixie had believed that she and Tor were getting really close, but how could she go on believing that comforting conviction when he continued to hide such a dreadful secret from her? His silence on that score hurt her a great deal, showing a dangerous fault line in their relationship, making her feel more insecure than ever about how he still viewed Katerina.

Tor was frowning now, his lean, strong features taut and a little forbidding. 'No, say whatever you have to say now.'

'I'll just spit it out, then,' Pixie murmured reluctantly. 'I found out some pretty shocking things listening to Dimitra this evening.'

'But you said—'

'I couldn't explain unless we had privacy,' Pixie interposed wryly. 'For a start, Katerina's parents are fully aware that their daughter was having an affair and was in the process of leaving you when she died. They tried to stop the affair, but she wouldn't listen to them.'

Tor was stunned.

'I can't credit that…are you sure?'

'Unequivocally. Dimitra actually said that pretending everything was fine in your marriage put more of a strain on them because they felt as though they were being forced to lie. But at the same time, she acknowledged that it was your right to maintain that pretence if that's what you preferred. She didn't have any axe to grind. I appreciate that you believed you were protecting them from distress by not telling them the truth but, really, I think it would have been easier all round if you'd just spoken up at the time,' she confided gently.

'You know nothing about it. I told you about the

situation with Sev though,' Tor bit out angrily, taking her aback because that anger seemed to come out of nowhere at her.

'According to your ex-mother-in-law, Sev *wasn't* Katerina's lover,' Pixie stated even more uneasily. 'It wasn't him, it was his brother, Devon.'

Tor stared back at her, his eyes dark with seething incredulity. 'That's not possible. Dimitra must have misunderstood.'

'I don't think so. They knew about the affair before you did and presumably, if they tried to stop it, they did discuss the man involved with their daughter,' Pixie pointed out quietly. 'Look, I know you hate all this being raked up again and I appreciate how difficult all of this is for you, Tor—'

'How the hell could you?' Tor demanded with ferocious bite. 'You're standing there giving forth about issues that are nothing to do with you and naturally I resent that.'

'I resent being plunged into the middle of your secret, sordid past when I didn't want to be involved in any way!' Pixie fired back at him, embarrassment and pain at his attitude combining to send her temper over the edge as well. 'As far as I'm concerned, I feel like Katerina might as well still be alive because you still think of her as your wife and protect her good name so carefully. Well, what about me? Where do *I* come in? I've only been married to you for a month and already I feel like I'm living in her shadow!'

'*Thee mou*...that's rubbish!' Tor blistered back at her, bronzed eyes shot through with smouldering lights of gold disbelief at that charge.

Pixie raised a doubting brow. 'Is it? Why are you still so guilty about her death that you took all the blame for it on your own shoulders? Were you a rotten husband? Were you unfaithful as well? And why didn't you tell me that Alfie was your *first* child? I feel that that's something that I should have known. Maybe because it's the only thing out of all of this mess that relates to me personally. But you should've told me that Sofia wasn't your daughter by blood. I understand and fully accept that you loved her and that you probably didn't discover that truth until Katerina was leaving you, but I do believe that you *could* have shared that with me.'

Tor had frozen where he stood, shaken at that hail of spontaneously emotional censure emerging from mild-tempered Pixie. 'I wasn't a rotten husband and I wasn't unfaithful. As to why I didn't tell you about Sofia's paternity...?' He spread lean brown hands. 'I can't really answer that. Maybe because it was the last straw, the ultimate humiliation for a man to learn that the child he has been raising and loving is not his. Maybe I was still in denial because, yes, I did love that little girl a great deal. But I still don't see how Sofia's paternity has anything at all to do with you or Alfie.'

'Well, that news doesn't surprise me,' Pixie retorted tight-lipped in her distress, furiously swallowing back the thickness in her throat and the warning sting at the backs of her eyes. 'All along you haven't once understood how I feel about anything because you don't really care about me. So, let's leave it there for tonight, Tor. I'm exhausted and I'm going to bed.'

'That's not true,' Tor declared as she snatched up her toiletries bag and cosmetics from the en suite and walked to the door. 'Where are you going?'

'I don't want to share a bed with you tonight. I don't want to be anywhere near you,' Pixie countered stiffly, determined not to reveal her distress in front of him. 'I'll sleep in one of the other cabins.'

'That's ridiculous… I don't want that. You're blowing this nonsense up out of all proportion,' Tor proclaimed rawly.

But Pixie didn't believe that. She was horribly upset, all her feelings flailing with pain inside her and he was the blind focus of them. And she didn't even know exactly what she wanted from him, only that she wasn't receiving it. Was she blaming him for not loving her as he had loved Katerina? She stopped dead in the empty cabin next door, stricken by that suspicion because that would be absolutely unfair to Tor. And she thought of what she had thrown at him without warning and almost cringed where she stood. When had she ever acted with so little compassion before? Where had her sympathy, her understanding gone?

Dear heaven, she had thrown in his teeth the reality that his poor little daughter had not been fathered by him. Had he even known that fact before she'd hurled it at him? Or had he only suspected that he might not be Sofia's father and had she confirmed his misgivings with her attack? Her stomach tightened and swirled with nausea at that possibility. She was horrified. Kicking off the high heels now pinching her toes, she trekked back barefoot to the master cabin.

A dim light glowed on the deck terrace beyond the French windows.

Through them she could see Tor leaning up against the rail, luxuriant black cropped hair ruffling in the breeze, his jacket discarded, the fine fabric of his shirt rippling against his lean, powerful torso, and her mouth ran dry the way it always did when the sheer beauty of him punched her afresh. Lifting her chin and suppressing that reaction, Pixie went outside to join him.

'Were you already aware that Sofia wasn't yours?' she pressed bluntly, her troubled face pale and tight in the low light.

Tor gritted his teeth. 'Yes… Yes, I knew. When I tried to prevent her mother from removing her from the house that night she told me then that Sofia wasn't my daughter. At first I didn't believe her because she was hysterical. But afterwards...' He breathed with difficulty. 'I had the tests done because I had to know the truth and it was confirmed.'

'I'm still really sorry I hurled it at you like that though,' Pixie muttered shakily. 'I also think that that little girl was very fortunate to have your love and care while she was alive. Like you, she didn't know the truth, but you loved each other anyway. You were still her father, Tor, in every way that mattered.'

Tor drained the tumbler in his clenched hand, whiskey burning down into the chill inside him because he was still in shock from their exchange. 'That's a really kind thing for you to say in these circumstances. But I'm sorry that you were inadvertently dragged into my secret, sordid past tonight. Just go to bed now, Pixie. I've got nothing else to say to you right now...'

And that was true. The tormenting belief that he could have wrongly believed his half-brother, Sevastiano, had betrayed him for so many years sickened Tor. In retrospect it struck him as unbelievable that he had chosen not to confront Sev. Did he blame his pride for that silence? His desire to let sleeping dogs lie for the sake of family unity?

Yet the instant Pixie had named Devon, pieces that had never made sense to Tor had locked together neatly to provide a much clearer picture of that secret affair. And suddenly, for the first time, it had all made sense.

Devon was Sev's English half-brother and he would already have been a married man when Katerina had first met him. No doubt that was why she had gone ahead and married Tor, because she had been unable to foresee and trust in a future with a lover who already had a wife and children. Easier access to Devon would explain why she had been so keen to live in London as well.

And Sevastiano?

Tor swore under his breath, recognising that his older brother would have been placed in an impossible situation, stuck in the middle between two half-brothers: one who had never really made an effort with him—Stand up, Tor, and own your mistakes, he urged himself—the other whom presumably he'd had a warmer relationship with because he had grown up with Devon.

How could Sevastiano possibly have chosen loyalties between them?

Dismissed, and feeling like a sleepwalker, Pixie went back next door, undressing where she stood, deciding that, yes, she could go to bed with makeup on because she didn't care, she really didn't care just at that moment. Her eyes were prickling and throbbing, the tears she had been holding back burning through her defences and finally overflowing, a painful sob tearing at her throat. He had thrown her own unjust words back at her…his 'secret sordid past'. And she should never have said such words to him when the sordid aspect had related to his wife's behaviour and had had nothing at all to do with his.

Why had she done it? Why had she dragged up all that messy stuff from the past and thrown it at him as though he were the worst husband in the world? And the easy answer twisted inside her like a knife and made her groan out loud because there was nothing very adult or admirable about her envy of Katerina, her possessive vibes about her son's status or her embittered attitude to Tor's grief over the death of his first wife.

In reality, she was a nasty jealous cow and now he knew it too. She had unveiled herself in all her immature, selfish glory for his benefit, all because she had admitted she loved him and he had ignored that confession. That disappointment had wounded her and put her in the wrong state of mind, releasing turbulent emotions that had quickly got out of her control. She had said things she didn't believe, demanded truths she wasn't entitled to receive and roused memories of a tragedy she truly hadn't wanted to bring alive for him again. And she had told him that she loved him and then acted in a very unloving way. Her eyes burned and ached as she recalled his tense chilliness towards her out on the terrace. Well, what had she expected from him? Bouquets and praise?

Tor stayed up thinking for most of the night and when dawn lightened the skies, he felt amazingly light as well. It had been so many years since he had felt like that that it was almost like being reborn. Reborn? Tor winced at that fanciful concept, but he was still smiling, still wondering how he had got everything so wrong for so very long and if it was even possible that he could have set a new record for sheer stupidity.

Pixie rose heavy-eyed in spite of the exhaustion that had finally sent her to sleep and grimaced at the tackiness of waking up without having removed her make-up. It sucked to have mascara ringing her eyes and smears of make-up on her pillow and she fully understood too late why she shouldn't have done it in the first place. She was in a funereal mood, eyes swollen and red behind strategically worn sunglasses, mouth tight, a wintry outfit chosen to suit her mood.

Tor surveyed her approach for an early breakfast, noting the jeans and the black sweater and how much they enhanced her petite yet curvy figure that drove him crazy with desire. Then there was the glorious glitter of her silky curls in sunlight and the sweet delicate lines of her troubled face. An uphill climb then, he recognised grimly, exactly what he deserved because he had done everything wrong, got everything wrong, merited nothing better.

In comparison to both parents, Alfie was brimming with energy and love. He bounced in his high chair with a huge smile at them both, held out his arms pleadingly to his mother, who for the very first time failed to notice his need, and succumbed to his father instead, who not only noticed but also swept him up and made him giggle and smile and gave him kisses.

'He needs to eat, Tor,' Pixie breathed curtly.

'He wanted a cuddle,' Tor breathed with perfect assurance. 'He's a very affectionate child. Sofia was much more reserved in nature.'

Disconcerted by that reference, Pixie lifted her head. 'She was?'

'Yes. Katerina kept us apart. I thought she was a possessive mother. Even when she kept me out of the delivery room when she was born I assumed the wrong things,' he told her, taking her utterly aback with those revelations. 'I didn't smell a rat.'

'A rat?' she echoed, nonplussed.

'I wasn't a suspicious husband,' he clarified wryly. 'But right from the beginning, she tried to keep me apart from Sofia. She knew she wasn't mine and she felt guilty.'

'Oh…' Pixie replied, her confusion only deepening at what could be driving his desire to be disclosing such facts when he had never been that confiding in relation to Katerina before.

'I didn't see it at the time. I didn't even see it afterwards,' Tor admitted starkly. 'I wasn't very good at seeing that sort of thing…in advance, as it were…or even in retrospect.'

'No, you're not very switched on that way… empathy-wise,' Pixie extended awkwardly. 'You're obviously very efficient in the business line, but in personal relationships you kind of lose the plot a little.'

'Or maybe don't even see the plot to begin with,' Tor added.

Pixie steeled herself to say what she still felt she had to say. 'I wasn't fair to you last night.'

'No, you got it right,' Tor broke in grimly. 'I got it wrong.'

That silenced Pixie, who had been trying to make amends without embarrassing herself. She didn't understand. She didn't want to get it wrong again either, though, and it was the fear of doing that that kept her quiet throughout their trip to the airport and their subsequent flight back to London.

'I want you to think about whether this house is right for us,' Tor remarked as the limo drew up outside the town house. 'I didn't buy it as a family house.'

'It's a blasted amazing house,' Pixie told him sniffily, because it was enormous and fancy and everything she believed suited him to perfection. 'It's even got a garden out back. What are you talking about?'

Tor mustered his poise and a decided amount of valour and breathed in deep and slow to say, 'Some day we may think of extending the family.'

Pixie sent him a wide blue-eyed glance of naked disbelief. 'Oh, you can forget that,' she said helplessly. 'Seriously, just forget that idea!'

Another baby? Was he kidding? Whatever, his expectations were seriously out of line with her own. She would be perfectly happy just to settle for Alfie…and…er…what? she asked herself. And she couldn't come up with a single goal because, in truth, without the love she craved, Tor had nothing to offer her. She was an unreasonable woman, she told herself squarely. He was gorgeous, amazing in bed and he did all the right things as if they had been programmed into him at birth. Seriously, he was the sort of guy who would never ever forget your birthday. It wasn't love but it was the best he could offer.

So, who was she to say it wasn't enough? Who was she in her belief that she ought to have more than the basics? This was a guy who had told her from the start that he didn't think he could fall in love again…that he could give her everything else but that.

Tor had been honest.

She had been dishonest, accepting him on those terms while secretly yearning for exactly what he had told her that he couldn't deliver. Appreciating that, she swallowed hard and struggled to suppress all the powerful hurt reactions that were making it virtually impossible for her to behave normally again with Tor. She had to stop acting that way, concentrate on the future he was holding out to her, not dwell on the downside, because everything had a downside to some extent. And that future Tor was suggesting included a larger family, which was something she would eventually want too, so why had she snapped at him when he admitted it?

Isla already had Alfie tucked in his crib when she entered the nursery.

The nanny was going home to stay with her own family for a few days and while Pixie loved and relied on having help with her son, she was, conversely, looking guiltily forward to having him all to herself again for a few days. Wishing the other woman a happy break, she went into the master bedroom, stiffening into immobility a few steps in when she glimpsed Tor poised by the tall windows.

'I have something I need to tell you,' he breathed as he swung round.

And Pixie wanted to run, didn't want any more stress, any more bad news. She was full to the brim and overflowing with insecurity, regret and worry as it was.

'This is important. Perhaps you should sit down,' Tor told her tautly. 'I may not be great in the empathy stakes, but I do know that we need to clear the air.'

And he was right, of course, he was, Pixie conceded, sinking down on the foot of the bed and folding hers arms defensively on her lap while watching him like a hawk to try and read his mood. But all she could read was his tension because his beautiful eyes were screened and narrowed in concentration. His uneasiness screamed at her because not since their very first meeting had she seen Tor look less than confident.

'What's wrong?'

'I finally worked some things out and it's changed the way I see everything,' he volunteered almost harshly. 'Try not to interrupt me. I'm not good at talking about this sort of stuff and I don't want to lose the thread of what I need to explain...'

'You're scaring me,' she whispered and then she clamped a guilty hand to her lips because she realised she had said that out loud even though she didn't intend to do so. 'Sorry.'

And for a split second his wide charismatic smile flashed across his serious features and her heart jumped inside her before steadying again, because nothing could be that serious if he could still smile like that. 'There's nothing to be scared of.'

Pixie nodded rather than speak again.

But the silence stretched way beyond her expectations as Tor paced with the controlled but restive aspect of a man who would rather be anywhere than where he was at that moment. His lean, impossibly handsome face went tight. 'I feel ashamed even saying it, but I can see now that Katerina and I didn't love each other the way we thought we did when we married, but that she had the misfortune of finding that out long before I did...'

Pixie was transfixed because whatever she had been expecting, it had not been that admission. She had always believed that Katerina had been his childhood sweetheart, his first deep love, his everything.

'There was no great passion between us. I didn't think that mattered. I assumed that being friends, getting on well, the similarity between our backgrounds and even our parents being so close was more than enough to make a really good marriage.' Tor shifted a pained lean brown hand. 'I was only twenty but considered mature beyond my years because I wanted to settle down and marry young. I thought I knew it all on the basis of very little experience. My parents tried to stop me, but I wouldn't listen to them either. I believed that what I felt for Katerina was love, but I can see now that it was more of a friendship, familiarity, admiration, loyalty, many decent things but not necessarily what a husband and wife need to stay together. I can only assume that it was the same for her and that when she met Devon, she quickly realised the difference.'

'Presumably, Devon wasn't initially prepared to leave his wife for her, or their affair wouldn't have lasted so long,' Pixie murmured uncertainly.

Tor shrugged. 'Who knows? But being able to finally see that different picture has made those events easier for me to accept. I think I felt so guilty about Katerina for so many years because in my brain somewhere, I knew I didn't love her the way she deserved to be loved.'

'But it was mutual, so you can't take on all the blame for that,' Pixie interposed soothingly, worried by his continuing tension. 'It's a very positive thing for you to be able to take a less judgemental view.'

'The guilt made it impossible for me to let go of the past. I felt responsible. I did care for her, but I shouldn't have argued with her that night.'

'No, stop it,' Pixie urged anxiously. 'No more blaming, no wishing you could change it all when you can't. Katerina made her choices as well and she chose to lie about everything. She chose not to tell you beforehand that she had fallen for another man or about Sofia. She drove off late at night in an emotional state of mind and that was the fatal decision which caused the accident.'

'I agree with you,' Tor admitted, startling her. 'It would never have happened as it did if she had not lied. I would have let her go, with great misgivings, but I would never have tried to keep her with me when she was unhappy and Sofia's paternity would have settled that. Be warned though...' Dark golden eyes locked to her hard and fast and her mouth ran dry. 'I would lock you up in a tower and lock myself in with you. I wouldn't be reasonable or compassionate or responsible. I would be possessive and enraged and jealous as hell!'

Pixie flushed and tilted her head back to look at him, blond curls tumbling back from her cheeks. 'And why would I get the tough treatment? Not that I'm thinking of straying,' she hastened to add.

Tor laughed half under his breath. 'The reason I finally understood that I didn't love Katerina was because I know what love feels like now. I've never been in love before, but it knocked me for six. For weeks since you came back into my life, I've been acting oddly because I didn't understand how I felt about you. So, while I was telling you that I couldn't fall in love again, I was actually falling in love for the first time, with you.' He grimaced. 'No prizes for my failure to recognise that happening. I'm not the introspective type. I don't analyse feelings, I just react, which is why I've been all over the place... emotionally speaking,' he completed with a harsh edge of discomfiture in his voice.

Pixie blinked, so shocked she wasn't quite sure what to say. He was telling her he loved her, a little voice screamed inside her head.

'I thought telling you would fix things!' Tor bit out in frustration. 'You love me... I love you. Isn't that enough?'

Pixie glided up out of paralysis like a woman in a dream because she was still telling herself off inside her head. He might not have known what he was feeling but she felt that she should have recognised in his desire to constantly be with her, to constantly touch her and connect, that he was feeling far more for her than a man merely striving to be an attentive partner. 'I've been blind,' she whispered. 'I was so envious of what I believed you must've felt for Katerina. It made me irrational. And yet I loved you anyway. I was always just wanting more.'

'Nothing wrong with wanting more.' Tor closed strong arms round her, dragging her close with the fierceness of his hold. 'But at the end of the day I just want you any damned way I can have you and it's much more powerful than anything I ever felt in my life before. I can't stand seeing you hurt or upset or unhappy,' he confided, crushing her soft parted lips under his with a revealing hunger that shot through her like a re-energising drug.

Clothes were discarded in a heap. His mouth still hungrily ravishing hers, he tugged her down onto the bed and drove into her hard and fast. The wild excitement engulfed her but there was a softer, more satisfying edge to it now because she knew he loved her. She felt safe, secure, happy, no longer sentenced to crave what she had believed she couldn't have because that had decimated her pride. Completion came in a climax of physical pleasure that shot through her in an electrifying high-voltage charge.

Afterwards, Tor cradled her close. 'I'll never forgive myself for not remembering you that day in my office.'

'No negative thoughts,' Pixie urged, fingers tracing his wide sensual mouth in reproach. 'We can't change the way we started out.'

'I think the absence of the green hair didn't help,' Tor teased. 'And I was more fixated by the fact that you were very pregnant, so I didn't look at you as closely as I should have done. But what I do understand is that we were incredibly lucky to find each other that first night because, for me, you are that one-in-a-million woman, who sets me on fire with a look. I love you so much...'

One in a million? That made Pixie feel good and she smiled up into the dark golden eyes welded to her with such fierce appreciation. 'Why didn't you respond when I told you I loved you?'

Tor laughed. 'Because I was a very late arrival to the party. I only realised last night. You talked of being in Katerina's shadow when you had never been and I sat up thinking about all of it, the past and the present. That's when what was really happening became clear to me. I understood how I truly felt after Katerina's death and why I hadn't got over that guilt. I also understood what I was feeling for you.'

'I probably would like another baby in a year or two,' Pixie told him, gently shooing away Coco, who was trying to climb into bed with them. 'Sorry I snapped over that idea. It's been a very emotional twenty-four hours.'

'But worth it,' Tor countered with a scorching smile, and he was bending his tousled dark head to toy with her lips again when a faint sound alerted Pixie and made her pull away from him.

'Alfie's awake.' Pixie slid off the bed and began to dress in haste. 'Isla's on holiday…remember?' she prompted.

'So, we get to be real parents,' Tor teased, rolling off the bed, naked and bronzed.

'Yes, Tor,' Pixie said with eyes filled with amusement. 'And the first lesson in being real parents is, you have to put on clothes.'

'Did I tell you how much I love you?' Tor asked, hitching an ebony brow.

'It was practically love at first sight for me.' Pixie held up a finger in unashamed one-upmanship. 'I win hands down.'

'I'm not so sure. I was a pushover for you and I'm not a pushover,' Tor declared. 'But maybe it was the green hair…'

'Well, we're never going to know for sure be-

cause I'm not going green again,' Pixie assured him
with a chuckle, bending forward to kiss him as he
pulled up his jeans and dallying there, Alfie having quieted again, her keen hearing assured her.

'And I'm never ever going to be without you
again, *agapi mou*,' Tor husked, gathering her to
him with all the possessiveness of a male determined never to let her go.

EPILOGUE

OVER TWO YEARS LATER, Pixie was presiding over a busy Christmas gathering at the mansion she and Tor had moved to overlooking the Thames. Surrounded by acres of gardens and possessed of numerous bedrooms, it was the perfect home for a family who enjoyed entertaining. Tor's relatives were frequent visitors.

Although that had not been her original intention, Pixie had never returned to work. At first, she had revelled in the luxury of being able to be with her son whenever she liked. But as she had begun to adapt to her new life, she had also become much busier. Having taken an interest in the charities that Tor supported, she had become actively involved with one in a medical field. She had soon realised that she could do a lot of good helping to raise funds and that fired up greater interest in such roles.

Moving from the town house into a much larger property had consumed a lot of her time as well, although she had thoroughly enjoyed the opportunity to decorate and furnish her first new home. That her first new home should be a virtual mansion still staggered her.

And now she was pregnant again, six months along and glowing with an energy she had not benefited from the first time around. Of course, she acknowledged, everything was different now for her. She was incredibly happy and secure and supported every step of the way. Tor's love had changed her, lending her new confidence and boosting her self-esteem. Discovering that she was carrying non-identical twins had been a bit of a shock at first, but a shock she and Tor had greeted with pleasure because they got so much joy out of Alfie, who was now a lively little boy of three.

Now she watched as Alfie dragged his grandfather, Hallas, outside to show the older man his ride-on car where it was parked on the terrace. Tor's father grinned as he visibly tried to explain in dumbshow to the little boy that he was far too big to get into the vehicle and take the wheel. Looking long-suffering with an expression that was pure Tor, Alfie climbed in instead to demonstrate his toy. Pixie smiled, feeling very fortunate that Tor's parents were so loving.

Tor had finally stopped being secretive about his first marriage and, although his revelations had roused shock and consternation, Pixie was inclined to believe that everyone was much more relaxed now that the truth was out and they were able to understand how Tor had felt for the five years that he had endured being treated like a heartbroken widower. Of course, he *had* been heartbroken in many ways, just not in the way that people had naturally assumed. She was particularly fond of her husband's half-brother, Sev, whom she had only got to know after Tor had cleared the air with him.

Just then she was wondering if Sev would manage to spend Christmas with them. Or if he was off somewhere else with some gorgeous beauty on a beach, drinking champagne and carousing, for Tor's Italian half-brother Sev was an unashamed womaniser, chary of any form of commitment and deeply cynical. Even so, he and Tor had eventually grown closer, in spite of the fact that at the start that development had looked unlikely.

A huge Christmas tree embellished the front entrance hall while a log fire crackled in the grate. Richly coloured baubles twirled at the end of branches decorated with glittering beaded strings, multicoloured reflections dancing off the marble hearth. It looked beautiful and so it should, Pixie conceded, because she had spent so much time seeking out special ornaments since her very first precious Christmas with Tor and Alfie. And every year she would bring them out and hang them, enjoying the memories that particular decorations evoked. Here and there on the branches hung the less opulent ornaments she had inherited from her late parents, enabling the tree to remind her of her happy childhood as well.

Her attention roamed to her brother, Jordan, where he was kneeling on the floor beside a little girl of about five. Tula was his girlfriend Suzy's daughter. It was a fairly new relationship, but Pixie was crossing her fingers and praying that it would work out for Jordan—because although he had rebuilt his life, she knew he needed someone to do it for and to ground him, and hopefully Suzy was that woman.

Jordan had suffered a long hard road in rehabilitation. There had been relapses and episodes of depression and various other obstacles for him to overcome, but in the end he had succeeded. He had found somewhere to live at his own expense and, a year ago, he had found work in a charitable organisation where he had no access to money. He had met Suzy through his job soon afterwards. Tor was very slowly warming up towards her sibling and generally becoming, under Pixie's influence, a little more compassionate with regard to other people's failings.

Tor came through the door with Alfie clinging

to him like a limpet while his father chatted to him, but Tor's stunning bronzed eyes sought out and instantly settled on his wife. There was a welter of talk and greetings as his entire family converged on him, for they had only arrived earlier that day and he had been at the office.

'My son adores you,' her mother-in-law, Pandora, pronounced with satisfaction at Pixie's elbow. 'You are the woman I always wanted for him and every woman deserves to be adored.'

'I adore him back,' Pixie whispered chokily.

'And another two grandchildren on the way together,' Pandora teased, fanning her face to lighten the atmosphere. 'What more can I say?'

'Three's enough!' Pixie laughed.

'We will see…'

Tor finally made it to Pixie's side. 'I need a shower and to change,' he groaned, raking his fingers up over his unshaven jaw with the attitude of a man suggesting that he resembled a down-and-out.

'Off you go,' his mother urged, her smile emerging as her son ensnared his wife's hand and tugged her upstairs with him.

'A shower?' Pixie lifted a dubious brow.

'Afterwards,' Tor suggested meaningfully, guiding her straight into their bedroom and peeling off his jacket in almost the same motion.

A pulse stirred between her thighs and turned

into an ache as she saw his arousal through the
fine expensive cloth of his trousers. It was a hunger that never quite dimmed. never ever got fully
satisfied, she acknowledged, studying him from the
crown of his cropped black hair to his shimmering
dark golden eyes to the electrifyingly sexy dark
shadow of stubble on his jawline. And something
gave within her and she just stepped forward and
flung herself at him with all the exuberant passion
that he revelled in.

'*Thee mou*... You are beautiful, *agapi mou*,'
Tor husked raggedly, struggling for breath as he
emerged from that kiss.

Not half as beautiful as he was, she thought, but
she had long since learned not to embarrass him
with such words of appreciation. 'This is going to
be a wonderful Christmas,' she told him happily.
'I feel so lucky. We've got everybody who matters
to us here to celebrate with us.'

'I really only need you,' Tor told her truthfully.
'And Alfie…and our twins,' he extended as he
turned her round and splayed large possessive hands
over the swell of her stomach. 'I never realised I
could love anyone the way I love you.'

'It was the green hair,' she teased.

'No, it was the first dynamite kiss. I'm a very
physical guy,' Tor breathed hungrily, divesting her
of her dress. 'Do you think we're having boys or

girls this time? I think boys because they seem to run in my family.'

'I think girls.'

They were both right. Three months later, Pixie gave birth to a boy and a girl, whom they christened Romanos and Zoe.

* * * * *

WE HOPE YOU ENJOYED
THIS BOOK FROM
⬡ HARLEQUIN
PRESENTS

Escape to exotic locations where passion knows no bounds.

Welcome to the glamorous lives of royals and billionaires, where passion knows no bounds. Be swept into a world of luxury, wealth and exotic locations.

8 NEW BOOKS AVAILABLE EVERY MONTH!

HPCNMRB1020

SPECIAL EXCERPT FROM

⟨H⟩ HARLEQUIN
PRESENTS

The hottest actor in Bollywood, Vikram Raawal has found love countless times—on-screen. In real life, he's given up on finding a soul-deep connection. Until at a masquerade ball, shy assistant Naina Menon leaves him craving more...

Read on for a sneak preview of Tara Pammi's next story for Harlequin Presents, Claiming His Bollywood Cinderella.

The scent of her hit him first. A subtle blend of jasmine and her that he'd remember for the rest of his life. And equate with honesty and irreverence and passion and laughter. There was a joy about this woman, despite her insecurities and vulnerabilities, that he found almost magical.

The mask she wore was black satin with elaborate gold threading at the edges and was woven tightly into her hair, leaving just enough of her beautiful dark brown eyes visible. The bridge of her small nose was revealed as was the slice of her cheekbones. For a few seconds, Vikram had the overwhelming urge to tear it off. He wanted to see her face. Not because he wanted to find out her identity.

He wanted to see her face because he wanted to know this woman. He wanted to know everything about her. He wanted... With a rueful shake of his head, he pushed away the urge. It was more than clear that men had only ever disappointed her. He was damned if he was going to be counted as one of them. He wanted to be different in her memory.

When she remembered him after tonight, he wanted her to smile. He wanted her to crave more of him. Just as he would crave more of her. He knew this before their lips even touched. And he would find a way to discover her identity. He was just as sure of that, too.

Her mouth was completely uncovered. Her lipstick was mostly gone, leaving a faint pink smudge that he wanted to lick away with his tongue.

She held the edge of her silk dress with one hand, and as she lifted it to move, he got a flash of a thigh. Soft and smooth and silky. It was like receiving a jolt of electricity with every inch he discovered of this woman. The dress swooped low in the front, baring the upper curves of her breasts in a tantalizing display.

And then there she was, within touching distance. Sitting with her legs folded beneath her, looking straight into his eyes. One arm held the sofa while the other smoothed repeatedly over the slight curve of her belly. She was nervous and he found it both endearing and incredibly arousing. She wanted to please herself. And him. And he'd never wanted more for a woman to discover pleasure with him.

Her warm breath hit him somewhere between his mouth and jaw in silky strokes that resonated with his heartbeat. This close, he could see the tiny scar on the other corner of her mouth.

"Are you going to do anything?" she asked after a couple of seconds, sounding completely put out.

He wanted to laugh and tug that pouty lower lip with his teeth. Instead he forced himself to take a breath. He was never going to smell jasmine and not think of her ever again. "It's your kiss, darling. You take it."

Don't miss
Claiming His Bollywood Cinderella,
available November 2020 wherever
Harlequin Presents books and ebooks are sold.

Harlequin.com